He wanted to fight for her. "Randolph would want you taken care of. He asked me to see that you were taken care of if anything should happen to him." Had Randolph sensed something? "I made a promise."

"Please let it be."

He didn't want to, but because she asked, he would. . . for now.

On the carriage ride back to her house, she said, "I'll write to William and ask him what he'd like to do about the house. Maybe he and Sarah will move up here. I think they'd like it here, don't you?"

What did it matter if William and his wife would like it here? "I'll write to William, as well, and tell him Randolph died before he could change his will. I know he will insist on honoring the new will, even unsigned."

"Don't. I won't accept it. Promise me you won't ask anything of William on my behalf."

"Why not?"

"I have my reasons. Please, Conner."

MARY DAVIS is a full-time writer whose first published novel was *Newlywed Games*. She enjoys going into schools and talking to kids about writing. Mary lives near Colorado's Rocky Mountains with her husband, three teens, and seven pets. Please visit her Web site at http://marydavisbooks.com.

Books by Mary Davis

HEARTSONG PRESENTS
HP399—Cinda's Surprise
HP436—Marty's Ride
HP514—Roger's Return
HP653—Lakeside
HP669—The Island
HP682—The Grand Hotel
HP690—Heritage
HP788—Uncertain Alliance

The Captain's Wife

Mary Davis

Heartsong Presents

In loving memory of my stepdad, Allen Basart.
Thanks for the history lesson, Dad.

A note from the Author:
*I love to hear from my readers! You may correspond with
me by writing:*

Mary Davis
Author Relations
PO Box 721
Uhrichsville, OH 44683

ISBN 978-1-59789-941-3

THE CAPTAIN'S WIFE

All scripture quotations are taken from the King James Version of the
Bible.

All of the characters and events in this book are fictitious. Any resem-
blance to actual persons, living or dead, or to actual events is purely
coincidental.

*Our mission is to publish and distribute inspirational products offering
exceptional value and biblical encouragement to the masses.*

PRINTED IN THE U.S.A.

one

Port Townsend, September 22, 1898

Leaning against the ornately carved mahogany mantel, Conner Jackson stared into the fire. The flames danced and licked at the logs like his guilt licked at his conscience. How could he have fallen for the wrong woman? In all his twenty-seven years of waiting, he thought he was smarter than that. He thought he could control his heart. Long ago, he told himself that he would leave town before coming between a friend and his lady. It was time to pull foot. Or as he'd once told his friend Ian MacGregor, he'd kick himself in the head. If he could figure out how, he'd do it.

"Here's your cider, Conner."

He turned to Mrs. Randolph Carlyle and took the amber liquid. "Thank you, Vivian." Guilt caused him to avoid her gaze lest his secret be revealed—he was in love with his best friend's new wife. His revelation twisted his gut.

Before Randolph had married, Conner had spent most of his time away from his store here at Randolph's house. He'd attempted to stay away after Vivian arrived to give the newlyweds some privacy, but Randolph wouldn't hear of it, insisting Conner spend time with him and his bride. Randolph seemed to need Conner to approve of his new wife, so he worked hard at getting to know her to give his friend an honest assessment. She was good for Randolph: a sweet, caring woman. Vivian had given Conner a warm welcome, treating him as a longtime friend she hadn't seen in years. He began to envy his friend's good fortune, wishing he'd met Vivian first.

Randolph clamped a hand on his shoulder. "Won't you have

something stronger? I have some fine brandy."

"I prefer the cider. It's fine, as well. You should try it."

Conner's longtime friend stood two inches shorter than his six-foot frame but was stockier and had a booming voice. For twenty years, they had looked after each other, seen each other through difficult times and good. Randolph was his best friend.

"Too sweet for my taste." Randolph stared into his glass but didn't take a drink.

Conner hoped his friend was reconsidering his drinking habits. He'd already cut back so much since marrying Vivian. Conner was praying Randolph would quit altogether.

Vivian sat like a regal princess, the epitome of decorum with porcelain skin, violet eyes, and raven black hair. A rare beauty, but her real beauty came from within. She was kind and generous and always had something good to say about everyone, including the riffraff in town.

The ripping ache in Conner's heart helped him with his difficult decision. He would make arrangements to leave town while Randolph was away. His store had done well with miners heading up to the Alaska gold rush, and he had plenty of money to start over someplace else. Maybe he would head south to Olympia.

"Randolph, you know what Conner needs?" Vivian's sweet voice drew him back. "A wife."

Dread clutched his gut. Did she suspect his affections for her? He groaned mentally.

Randolph took a drink of his brandy. "I believe if Conner wanted a wife, he could have any single lady in town to choose from. Isn't that right, Conner?"

He grimaced at the truth in the crass remark. Ladies had always thrown themselves at him and made it very clear that they were available to him, married or not. Those kinds of women held no appeal. "The women around here are a bit too bold for my taste."

"My point, exactly, Randolph. We need new blood in town. Do see what you can do about bringing him back a suitable lady."

Randolph guffawed. "You don't just land in port and pick up a lady."

"You did." She smiled at her husband, and Conner's heart tripled its beat. She was always generous with her smile and made anyone feel welcomed.

Randolph smiled back at his wife and raised his glass to Conner. "What do you say? Shall I bring you back a bride?"

"No, thank you." He wanted to tell his friend that he wouldn't be around when he returned but knew Randolph would try to talk him out of leaving and would insist on knowing why he was pulling foot. He would never tell Randolph that he fancied his wife. It was just plain wrong. The only way to stop this, or at least to control it, was to vamoose. Randolph had been the one to talk him into starting his general store in Port Townsend and would be disappointed when he was gone.

Vivian sat forward. "Oh, Conner, please. It would be so much fun if you had a wife; then she and I could be friends, and the four of us could dine together and throw parties." Vivian had had trouble making friends in town. She didn't behave like the other ladies of the town's proper society. She didn't value people based on how much money they had. She valued people simply for being people. Consequently, the members of the town's elite hadn't given her a warm welcome.

She made solving his problem sound simple. Get a wife and live happily ever after. But not if he didn't love the woman and he was in love with another man's wife. Maybe he wasn't so much in love with Vivian as he coveted Randolph's happiness. Either way, leaving town was the best option. "I should be going." And not just from Randolph's house. He set his cider aside and stood.

"A toast first." Randolph held his glass high. "To Vivian,

my lovely wife, a more virtuous wife you will never find." He drank down the last of his brandy.

A hint of sadness in Vivian's eyes twisted Conner's heart. What could possibly cause her sorrow? She had everything she could want. Couldn't Randolph see her distress?

It wasn't his place to bring it up or to comfort.

&

Vivian sat at her dressing table, removing the pins from her hair. Randolph hadn't said his loving wife or the wife he loved and adored, but his lovely wife. Once again it was her beauty he saw, her body he desired. Could he ever truly love her? Not if he thought she was his virtuous wife but found out she was once one of the lowliest of sinners.

Randolph caressed her hair and held it in his fingers. "I never imagined hair could be this silky." He looked over her shoulder and gazed at her reflection. "You are so beautiful."

Though the compliment saddened her, she gave him a small smile. What she knew he expected. "Thank you, Randolph."

She pulled her hair over her shoulder and stroked it with her sterling silver brush. Married only three months, she didn't know her husband well. They had married two days after they had met in Coos Bay, Oregon. Then they arrived in Port Townsend, and he'd been out to sea much of the time. He was a good man but haunted by his childhood. She realized now her error in her haste to latch onto the security of marriage. Her secret would eventually tear them apart. How could they love each other with her past standing between them? William had sternly warned her never to tell his brother what she had done.

When William and Randolph's father had died, their mother had turned to prostitution for a while to feed and clothe her two boys. Randolph had never forgiven her.

She gazed at her reflection. Only twenty-five, she felt as though she'd lived two lifetimes. She shifted her gaze to Randolph's reflection. "When do you head down to your ship?"

"In a few hours, but I want to spend some time with my wife before I leave." Randolph raised her to her feet and turned her to him. "My exotic beauty." He captured her mouth.

Is that all he could see? Her heart cried out for more. For love.

His lips traveled across her cheek, and he stopped. "What is this, tears?" He caressed them away with his thumbs.

She hadn't realized her tears had escaped. She turned away from him and dried the rest of her face with her hands. "I'm going to miss you."

He turned her back. "These aren't the tears of a wife missing her husband before he leaves. What's upsetting you?"

She should tell him. William's warning rushed back to her. *He will never accept your past. Never!* "Nothing, really."

His expression hardened as did his grip on her arms. "Tell me."

"Randolph, that hurts."

He jerked his hands away, horror twisting his face. "I'm sorry." He knelt in front of her and took her hand, kissing it. "Forgive me."

"Please get up." She hated seeing him grovel. Not to her. Never to her.

He stood. "I promised myself I would never hurt a woman or child. I don't know what came over me. I'll never do it again. You have my word."

"Sometimes we find ourselves doing things we never thought we would." *Becoming a person we don't want looking back at us in the mirror.*

"Not you. You are a perfect wife, a perfect lady."

She turned away from him to hide her shame. "I am far from perfect."

He stepped in front of her. "Look at you. Everything about you is perfect. Every lady would want to look as you do. What small imperfection do you think you have?"

See more in me than physical beauty, her heart cried. "I am more than outward appearance."

With a finger under her chin, he lifted her face. "Why the tears tonight?"

He blurred in front of her.

"Have I done something to upset you?"

She blinked the tears back. "I don't want to spoil things before you leave."

His mouth turned up in a kind smile through his whiskers. "You are too good for me."

She couldn't stand his misconceptions any longer and stepped back from him. Her red taffeta dress rustled. "No, Randolph. It is you who are too good for me. I am not worthy to be your wife. I'm not worthy of you at all." She couldn't harbor this secret any longer. Like a slow-burning ember, it was consuming her newfound faith a little at a time. Even if it destroyed them both, he had a right to know. "I am not the lady you think I am. I'm a harlot. Or at least I was." She let the words rush out before she could change her mind, then held her breath.

He took a step back and frowned. "That isn't true. You can't be."

She reached out to him as a child would for understanding, but he moved out of her reach. "I was a widow and had nothing. I was hungry and cold and had no place to live. A man was kind to me. I didn't know the Lord Jesus. I didn't know it was so wrong. But Jesus changed me. I no longer lived like that when you met me. Friends helped me. Believe me, I would never go back to that. Never."

He gritted his teeth and his face flamed red. "Friends? What friends?"

She shrunk away from his booming voice. "It doesn't matter."

His features hardened even more, and his tone turned accusatory. "My brother and his wife."

A tear slipped down her cheek. "I want to be a good wife to

you. What does my past matter? I am a new creation in the Lord Jesus Christ."

His face twisted into a snarl. "You deceived me. Made me believe you were a proper lady. Was marrying me just another harlot trick?"

"No, Randolph. I truly was trying to make a new start. I never meant to hurt you. I want to be a good wife to you. I want you to really love me, but it wasn't going to be possible with my secret between us."

"Love a harlot? Not likely." He strode out of their bedroom, slamming the door behind him.

She jerked it open, refusing to be dismissed. She caught up to him by the front door. "Please forgive me. Please." There had to be a way to salvage the remains of her short marriage. "I am the lady you married and a new creation. God has forgiven my past. Can't you?"

"A lady would never sell herself. Never. You deceived me to get me to marry you." He swung on his captain's overcoat and hat. "I'll deal with you when I return."

She reached out for his arm. "Please, Randolph, forgive me."

He pulled from her grasp. "Don't touch me." He slammed the door on his way out.

She covered her eyes and cried. *Sweet Lord Jesus, please let him forgive me.*

An arm wrapped around her shoulder. "Come, dear. He'll return soon." Maggie, the cook and housekeeper, guided her back upstairs and helped her change for bed.

❧

Conner woke in the middle of the night to the slurred bellowing song of a drunk out on the street. He wanted to ignore it, but he recognized that song and the singer's voice. He pulled on his pants and a shirt. "Come on, Fred."

Fred cocked one brown scruffy ear from where she lay in a circle on the end of his bed.

"Come on, girl."

The little terrier stood and stretched from her nose all the way down to her hind legs then jumped off the bed.

People often wondered about giving a boy name to a girl dog, but it was just one of those things that happens. When he'd seen the cold, dirty, wet stray wandering the streets of Seattle, the name Fred immediately popped into his head and fit. He'd soon realized Fred was a girl but kept the name. At least that's what he told people. The story of how as a lonely little boy he had been refused the comfort of a pet by a mother who hadn't wanted her own son, let alone a dog named Fred, was not a good tale. His mother had kicked the dog and sent it away. Conner never saw Fred again. Over the years, he'd wondered what had happened to that dog. So when another stray entered his life, it only seemed natural to name her Fred.

He headed downstairs and through his store, with Fred on his heels.

Randolph sat on the boardwalk step outside. Drunk as a skunk. This had been his normal pattern when he was in port: to get drunk at least one night and end up here. But since he'd married Vivian, he'd not spent one night sleeping off a drinking binge in Conner's back room. What had changed things tonight? Had he fought with Vivian? Conner looked toward uptown. Was she in as bad shape as Randolph?

He'd been friends with Randolph since he was seven, Randolph was ten, and Randolph's brother was five. The three had run barefoot around the streets of San Francisco together. Or at least the streets of their block. Randolph's mother had combed their hair and made them go to church every Sunday. Conner's mother had done her best to ignore the fact that she'd produced a child. "Come inside, old friend."

Randolph turned toward Conner's voice and waved his bottle at him. "Sit down. Have a drink. 'S good whiskey."

Both Randolph and Conner had accepted Jesus Christ as their Savior when they were boys. But unlike Conner, who had pressed harder toward the Lord when trouble came, Randolph had turned his back and had been running ever since. No matter what Randolph said or did, Conner knew that the Lord had not turned His back on the crusty sea captain. When Randolph was ready, he would see that God had been waiting with open arms the whole time to welcome back His prodigal child. And Randolph wasn't so far away; he'd gone to church twice with Vivian. The only two Sundays he'd been in town.

Conner sat but refused the whiskey. "You should come inside so you don't disturb those trying to sleep."

Randolph groped the railing and awning post to pull himself to his feet and started staggering. "I have to be on my ship. I'm the captain. My men need me."

Heading in his current direction, Randolph wasn't going to make it to his ship, so Conner turned his friend toward the dock. "This way."

Randolph poked him in the chest. "Don't ever trust women. Not ever. You can't trust 'em. They're all bad." He waved his bottle in the air. "All of them." He sighed and quieted.

What had happened tonight after he'd left? Randolph must have fought with Vivian. Conner hoped it wasn't over finding him a wife. He didn't want to come between the two of them, not ever. It was good that he'd be leaving town. "Wait here while I lock up, and I'll walk you to your ship." He locked his store door and quickly returned to his swaying friend.

"You're a good friend, Conner. You always were." Randolph patted him on the chest with his palm. "Promise me you'll look after her until I return. Look after Vivian."

That was the last thing he should do. The fox guarding the henhouse? Oh, what trouble could be had. He looped his arm around his friend to help him walk.

"Look after her, but don't get any ideas about her. Don't you touch her. I should have known she was too beautiful to trust. Don't you ever touch her."

"I promise not to touch her." That was one promise he could make and vow to keep. Vivian was another man's wife—his friend's wife. He could never touch her.

"And you'll guard her while I'm gone."

Guard? He struggled to keep Randolph on his feet.

"Promise me."

"I promise, Randolph." If Vivian stayed uptown and he remained downtown, that should be easy enough to keep.

Randolph seemed to sober and spoke clearly. "If anything happens to me, you'll see that she's all right."

"Nothing's going to happen to you." Conner staggered under the weight of his friend. "You're the finest captain on the sound and all the West Coast."

Randolph stopped in the middle of the dock and grabbed Conner by the front of his coat. "Promise."

He wanted to shout no, but what reason could he give his friend for not being willing to honor this simple request? He gritted his teeth. "I promise." As soon as Randolph's ship was spotted on the horizon, Conner would pull foot.

He loosened Randolph's grip on his coat and hailed the first mate. "Help me get your captain to his cabin." He and the first mate supported Randolph to his cabin and laid him on his bed. Conner said nothing more to the first mate as nothing needed to be said. He patted his leg to the scruffy brown terrier at his feet. "Come on, Fred, let's go home."

At his store, he went upstairs to his living quarters and gazed out the back window at the sparkling water in the moonlight and laid his head upon the cold glass. It was not good to test temptation. "Lord, what have I done making such promises? I will leave as soon as Randolph sets foot back in Port Townsend. Help me to honor my promises to an old friend while still honoring You."

two

Thunder cracked and rolled across the sky, startling Vivian awake. A storm. Good. They could use the rain. It had been three weeks since they'd gotten a drop. And a week since Randolph had left. He would be pleased if his roses got the water they needed. Maybe it would soften his mood when he faced her. She climbed from bed, slipping on her dressing robe before stepping out onto her balcony. Most people called it a widow's walk, but it was only that if a widow was on it, in her opinion. The air was heavy with humidity, but no rain fell yet, the rolling black clouds begging for release.

She shouldn't have told Randolph the truth. William had warned her. But her secret had weighed so heavy on her; she couldn't stand it. What would he do to her when he returned? Would he beat her? Send her away? A tear slipped down her cheek as she remembered Randolph's disgust with her before he left. Would she get a chance to make amends with him?

Lord, please let Randolph see that I can be a good wife to him. Forgive me for keeping this secret from him. I just wanted to start over. I wanted to be the person Randolph thought I was.

The first huge drop of rain splashed onto her hand. She gripped the cold metal railing and turned her face to the sky as the clouds gave up their bounty, washing her in refreshing cool water. But the rain that watered and gave life would also turn the streets to mud, and people would grumble about the lack of sunshine. She let the rain cleanse her, but it couldn't touch her inside. Jesus had forgiven her and cleansed her soul. Could Randolph forgive her, as well?

❧

Vivian cut the quarter chunk of the ten-inch Colby cheese

wheel into five pieces, wrapped the bundle in a cheese cloth, and put it in her basket along with five apples and five biscuits. "Maggie, would you hand me those stale bread crusts for the seagulls?"

The cook held out the paper sack Vivian had been collecting the bread in; then she peered into Vivian's nearly full basket. "Those are mighty hungry birds."

Vivian put the sack into her basket and covered it with a yellow checkered cloth. "That they are."

"We got a couple of young roosters in this last batch of laying hens. They're causing a fuss chasing around my hens. Maybe I'll just butcher them and fry them up. You think those birds of yours like fried chicken?"

Vivian kissed Maggie on the cheek. "They would love it."

"You be careful now. Anything happens to you, and the captain will be butchering me."

That might have been true two weeks ago before Randolph left, but now if something were to happen to her, Randolph might be relieved. He could be the grieving widower captain, and no one would ever find out about his poor choice in a wife. How would he choose to "deal with her"? Maybe it would be best if she weren't here when he returned.

She gazed at Maggie's concerned face and, remembering the cook had admonished her to be careful, patted her skirt pocket. "I have my Derringer. I'll be fine." After all, she was going downtown in the middle of the day. Unfortunately, she had experience in handling unruly men.

She walked the blocks to the steep narrow stairs that connected uptown with its respectable residents and her new station in life to downtown and a reminder of her old life. She descended to the bustling streets below past people who did hard physical labor to put food on their family's table, miners who were passing through on their way to Alaska to make their fortune, seadogs who were grateful to be on land for a few hours, and the dozens of other good people trying to make their way. The common people of downtown stared at her, and she smiled back. She traveled along the main street and climbed down the wooden steps to the beach, where the air became even saltier. She stepped carefully over the uneven rocks to the drift log and sat.

With her basket beside her, she began throwing bread-crumbs to the gathering seagulls. Through the squawks of the gulls, she heard crunching in the rocks behind her and smiled. It never took them long. They didn't have much else to do but wait for her to come. Five dirt-smudged faces stared expectantly at her. All the children had tears in their clothing, and none of them had bathed or combed their hair in a long time.

She had discovered these homeless orphans a week ago when she'd come down to the beach to contemplate her future after Randolph's return. With no local orphanage, these children were left to fend for themselves. The good people of uptown had no idea there were any needy children or any needy people at all. They preferred to remain on their safe streets away from the harsh realities of life, thinking everyone lived in the same kind of proper, perfect world they'd sequestered themselves to. They thought that only rough miners heading north to the Alaska gold fields were on the streets below. They didn't want to know about needy families, women, and children. They preferred to live in their utopian world, looking to the salty water beyond without seeing the riffraff below.

She held out her hands to Samuel on one end and Peter on the other, forming a circle. Together they all recited, "Thank You, Jesus, for this food. Amen."

"What did you bring uth?" Peter, five years old and the youngest of the bunch, had brown loopy curls and a smile that would one day melt hearts. And, she noticed, he had developed a lisp.

Betsy shook Peter by the shoulder. "Pipe down. That ain't

polite." At ten and the only girl in the bunch, she'd taken on mothering all four boys—even the two older ones.

"Oh, she don't mind." Peter jumped up onto the log next to her. "Do you, Mith Vivian?"

"Betsy is right. If you want to find a good home, you need to have proper manners." She smiled at the boy. "But I don't mind." She put her basket on her lap and pulled back the yellow cloth.

All five children sucked in an audible breath. She handed them each a chunk of cheese, a red apple, and a biscuit. They took the food greedily.

Peter handed back the apple. "I cain't eat no apple." The boy turned to her, bared his teeth, and pushed one of his front teeth straight out with his tongue.

It wasn't hanging on by much and was the reason for his newly acquired lisp.

George, the oldest at fourteen, held out his biscuit to Peter. "Trade?" These kids looked out for each other. They were all each other had.

Peter eagerly swapped his shiny red apple for the fluffy biscuit. If Peter worried about eating the apple with his loose tooth, he'd also have a hard time with the cheese.

She didn't want him to go hungry on account of his fear over a loose tooth. "Why don't you let me pull that tooth for you?"

Peter pinched his mouth shut and spoke through pursed lips. "No, ma'am."

"It will be easier to eat."

He shook his head hard, brown curls flopping back and forth.

She reached in her skirt pocket past her little gun and pulled out a penny. "I'll trade you this penny for your tooth."

Peter's eyes widened as he stared at the copper coin. He reached into his mouth and pinched his eyes closed as tight as he could get them. He pulled just a bit and held up the tooth in triumph. "Hey, that didn't hurt." Then he quickly swapped it for the penny.

"You're a brave little boy."

Peter danced around, holding up his prize. "I goth a penny. I goth a penny."

She noticed George, Samuel, and Tommy staring at the penny. She pulled out five more pennies, leaving four in her pocket, and gave them each one with Peter getting a second one. She would get another penny from home and give them each another one tomorrow when she brought them Maggie's fried chicken. The children scattered on the beach to eat.

She looked around at the four older children sitting on the smooth sand that was closer to the water's edge. George was fourteen and nearly a man. Samuel was twelve, Betsy ten, and Tommy nine. Samuel and Tommy were the only two who were related. She worried about Betsy the most. The boys would eventually find jobs like George had done. Girls had a harder time finding a decent job at a young age. There were two options for Betsy when she got older: find a husband while she was still a girl or become a. . . Vivian had to do something to help these children. Food was fine for now, but what would they do when the weather turned cold?

The days were already getting cooler. She wanted to take them home but knew Randolph would never approve of orphans running loose in his house. She didn't even know what would become of her when her husband returned to "deal" with her. She'd liked the idea of having a husband to care for and protect her, but now it was a bit scary having her fate in the hands of someone else.

She stood and went to Betsy, draping the yellow gingham cloth from the basket over the girl's shoulders. "That's for you."

"Thank you, Miss Vivian."

"Do you know how to sew?" Not that her sewing ability was very good nor had helped her when she was in need those years ago, but maybe Betsy would have better luck, and she would be praying for the girl to get a respectable job. Maybe if someone had been praying for her, things would have turned out differently.

Betsy tipped her head up and shook it. "I never had a mama to show me."

"I'll bring some dry good squares tomorrow and teach you." If the girl took to it, well, maybe she could get a job sewing or mending when she was a little older.

When the children had finished their cheese and tucked their apples and biscuits into their pockets for later, they headed back to wherever they had come from. Vivian wished she could do more for them, but when Randolph returned, she might not be able to do anything for them anymore. Would she be as destitute as they? She knew what that was like.

She headed back up through town, and as she walked, she noticed a man in a Stetson. He tipped his hat back, staring at her openly. She crossed to the other side of the street. He followed and stepped in her path. "Well, aren't you a purdy thing."

She tried to sidestep the man, but he blocked her.

Heavy footsteps rushed up behind her. Her heart thumped hard in her chest. His friend, perhaps? Reaching into her pocket, she wrapped her fingers around her Derringer. Only one bullet. Maybe she could scare them off with it.

A sinister voice came from behind her. "You lay one hand on Mrs. Carlyle, and I'll have to kill you."

The cowboy held up his hands and backed away. "I'm sorry, mister. Didn't mean no harm to your missus."

She turned and smiled at Conner.

Conner's gaze and pistol remained on the retreating man. When the man was a safe distance away, Conner lowered his gun and turned his glare on her. "What are you doing down here? It's not safe for a lady to be downtown. Do you know the kind of people who are down here? Miners and strumpets and people like that man and worse."

If he knew she had been one of those kinds of people he'd just described, he'd be just as disgusted as Randolph. She released her grip on her gun. "I came to see you." He would only scold her further if he knew she had been down at the water, alone. Not exactly alone.

The V between his eyebrows deepened. "You shouldn't have come. If you needed something, you should have sent someone to get me."

&

"Let's get you off the street." Conner guided Vivian back to his general store, careful not to touch her.

"How did you know to come to my rescue?"

The lilt in her voice tickled his ears. "I saw him follow you across the street." He'd grabbed his gun from his holster behind the counter and left. "Martin went out to get himself lunch." Martin Zahn had worked for him for eighteen months. Before that, Conner had had a slew of dishonest men work for him. He had a couple of other all right fellows who worked for him on occasion. "When he returns, I'll see you home safely."

"That's not necessary. I can walk by myself."

"You walked down here?" Was she crazy? "That cowboy wasn't going to stop at how-do-you-do." Was she so innocent that she didn't realize some people had ill intentions? Her acceptance of all people regardless of their background was one of the things that drew him to her.

"Can I get a little help here?" A customer called.

He resisted the urge to growl. "I'll be right with you." He turned to Vivian. "You'll be safer waiting in the back."

"I don't want to go in the back."

He did growl now. "Then sit on that stool behind the counter." He walked her over then looked down at his dog. "You keep an eye on her, Fred." The dog sat next to the stool. He went to attend to his customer. He waited on several more people before Martin returned. When he reached Vivian, she had Fred on her lap and the Sears and Roebuck catalog open on the counter in front of her.

"I'll walk you home now."

She turned to him. "I want to order from the catalog."

His heart hammered hard at her smile. "You can shop at plenty of places uptown, and I'm sure one of them has a catalog."

"But I want to order from you, my husband's dear old friend."

If Randolph knew the feelings he had for his wife, Conner wouldn't be his friend anymore. He pulled out a sheet of paper. "What do you want?" The sooner he got this over with, the sooner he could get her home and away from his temptation.

Vivian named several things. "Let me know when those come in."

"I'll have them delivered to your house. Can we go now?" He needed to get away from her, and to do that, he had to get her back uptown where she belonged.

Vivian held out her hand for him to assist her off the stool. He took it grudgingly, soft and delicate, then dislodged his hand from hers and turned to Martin. "Would you prepare this order and send it?"

On the walk to uptown, Conner kept his hands clasped tightly behind his back and took in slow, controlled breaths. Randolph would be back soon, and then Conner would leave for good. Just a little longer, and he'd be free.

When they reached Randolph and Vivian's blue Victorian house, she said, "You must be parched. Won't you come in and have a cup of tea with me?"

His mouth was drier than all get-out, but the last thing he needed to do was socialize with his friend's wife, who made him wish for things he had no business pining for. Trouble, that's what it all was, downright heart-wrenching grief any way you sliced it. "I have to get back to my store. Stay uptown," he ordered.

"Conner, you worry too much." She touched his arm, and he flinched.

Better to be on his guard and worry too much than not enough and get himself in a heap of trouble. He tipped his hat to her, patted his leg for Fred, who seemed a little confused about who to go with, and left. Once back on the street, he could breathe again. He had to maintain control and distance.

Vivian's gentle smile and kindness had lassoed his heart as proficiently as if she were an experienced cowhand. And she didn't realize it. He'd seen so many men who would cut off their right arm for a lady who was nice to them. He hadn't thought he was one, but Vivian's sweet nature and acceptance of him without question had dragged him down to a place he didn't want to be. In love with his best friend's wife. She didn't mean to make him fall in love with her, but here he was, the worst kind of man. He would be leaving soon, and it would all get a lot easier.

three

Shortly after Conner returned from Vivian's, Finn came into his store, scratched his whiskers, made eye contact, and headed to the back room. Finn was a strange character in his late fifties with well-worn clothes that bordered on rags.

Conner finished the customer's purchase and found the old drifter with a cup, drinking the dregs from the coffeepot. "Why the long face?"

Finn had come with Conner over from Seattle two years ago. The old codger helped out when he needed money or food, but mostly just hung around to jaw with the miners as they came through. "I have news."

Finn heard the strangest stories. Conner only believed about half of them. Tall tales were common in port towns. He didn't think Finn believed most of the stories either, but the older man liked to tell them anyway. "What news?"

Finn swiped his mouth with his shirtsleeve. "About your friend, the captain."

Finally, Randolph was back, and Conner could pull foot. "When does he dock?"

"He don't."

"What?" That didn't make sense. Randolph should have returned two days ago.

"He was making a run up to Alaska with keg powder and dynamite. The story goes that he was just off the coast when a storm come up. Lightning struck the ship. They say the captain ordered his men to abandon ship. Some of 'em did, but some of 'em stayed and helped the captain try to put out the fire before it reached the cargo hold. It lit up the western sky when it blew, the people on land said."

"Randolph?"

Finn nodded. "Men say he was still working the fire when it went up."

"No." Conner raked his hand through his hair. "Are you sure?"

Finn handed him an Alaskan newspaper. The front-page picture showed something burning on the horizon of the water with a lightning bolt streaking across the sky.

Finn's story wasn't just hearsay from the sailors but news. Conner blinked back tears as he read. There was no hope of Randolph making it. "I have to tell Vivian. Can I take this?"

૨૭

Vivian turned the apple in her hand, spiraling off the peel with a paring knife as she created one long strip. Maggie was making applesauce to can. She hadn't tasted Maggie's applesauce before, but if it was anything like her other cooking, it would be delicious.

Scotty, their handyman, entered the kitchen with his old hat pressed to his chest. He acted as butler when he was near, groundskeeper, stableman, and anything else Randolph or Maggie needed him for. But mostly, Randolph let the old man live out his remaining years doing only the jobs he chose to do.

Scotty was stoop-shouldered and had a weathered face. If she had to guess, Vivian would say he was in his seventies. "Mr. Jackson's here to see you, ma'am. I put him in the parlor."

Had he come to scold her again? She stood to walk out of the kitchen.

"Where do you think you're going?" Maggie wiped her hands on her apron.

"To see Conner."

"Not like that." Maggie untied Vivian's apron.

"It's only Conner, my husband's dearest friend, who doesn't care what I look like."

"You are the wife of Captain Carlyle." Maggie rolled down

the sleeves of Vivian's white blouse and buttoned the cuffs. "You must always look proper. It would be no good if word got back to the captain that you were working in the kitchen. He'd turn me out on the street."

Randolph would never get rid of Maggie, but since he already had enough to hold against her, Vivian let Maggie fuss over her and tuck in a hair or two. Maybe if she showed her husband she could be a proper wife to him despite her background, he wouldn't turn her out and would one day come to love her. She stepped away from Maggie and held out her hands. "That's quite enough. I'm sure I'm presentable."

She went straight to the parlor. "Conner, so good to see you."

Conner turned from where he stood by the window, ashen faced, his expression bleak. "Sit, Vivian."

Her stomach constricted. "What is it?"

He came around the sofa with a newspaper tucked under his arm. "Sit."

She didn't want to sit. Conner loomed six inches taller over her, and she sank back onto the sofa. "Tell me." Her stomach pinched into a tight ball, and her heart struggled to beat at the sight of Conner's serious countenance.

❧

Conner hated being the one to break Vivian's heart with bad news, but better him than a stranger. "It's Randolph." He swallowed hard. "His ship went down."

She gasped. "No. Is he all right?" She stood. "Take me to him."

He took her elbow and lowered her back to the sofa. "He didn't make it."

Her hand flew to her mouth.

He unfolded the paper.

She gasped. "Is that. . . ?"

"His ship? I'm afraid so." He wished it weren't.

She took the paper in a shaky hand and stared at the grainy photo taking up most of the front page. "It shouldn't have been him. It should have been me."

What was she saying? The shock must be confusing her. Conner fisted his hands as he watched the agony play on her face. "Maggie." He wanted to hold her and comfort her, but he knew he couldn't. "Maggie!"

Maggie entered and looked from Vivian to him. "What have you done to her?" She sat next to Vivian and wrapped an arm around her.

He stared at the woman sitting where he wanted to be. "Captain Carlyle is dead."

Vivian's gaze remained on the photo.

Maggie glared at the paper, then up at him. "Take that away."

He folded the paper and slipped it back under his arm.

Vivian's confused gaze followed the paper then traveled up to his face. "It shouldn't be this way. He shouldn't be dead. Maybe he got off."

Maggie looked to him.

He shook his head.

"Let's get you up to bed." She helped Vivian stand and ushered her out of the room.

He turned to Scotty, who stood silently near the doorway. "If she needs anything, come get me. If any of you need anything. I'll come by tomorrow and see how she's doing."

※

The next morning, Conner shuffled around the kitchen area of the small living quarters above his store. He still couldn't believe that Randolph wasn't coming back. Was there any way he could have survived? He unfolded the newspaper and stared at the photograph, then shook his head. Anyone on that ship when the powder went up hadn't had a chance. The concussion from the explosion alone would have rendered anyone nearby unconscious. If they had lived through the blast—whether they were thrown from the ship or not—they would have drowned. His friend was gone, and he had to accept that.

He rubbed his face as he headed downstairs and to the

front where Fred sat. "So that's where you went." After he'd let the dog out the back this morning and inside again, Fred had remained downstairs. Conner raised the shade and froze in the middle of unlocking the door. Scotty stood leaning against the awning post. Conner quickly opened the door. "Scotty, what is it?"

"Miss Maggie's in a terrible state. She doesn't know what to do with Mrs. Carlyle. She's been out on that widow's walk all night. Wouldn't let Maggie bring her in. All Maggie could do was wrap a quilt about her."

"My assistant will arrive soon; then I'll come straight away. You return and let Maggie know I'm coming." He wasn't sure what he was going to be able to do. If Vivian wouldn't come inside for Maggie, she wasn't likely to for him, either. But he would do something neither Maggie nor Scotty would; he'd physically carry her inside if he had to.

As he strode up to the house a half hour later, he could see Vivian on the widow's walk in the same green skirt and white blouse she had worn yesterday, her gaze firmly fixed on the water's horizon. What must she be thinking? He hoped nothing dire.

The door opened before he reached it. Maggie clutched her hands to her chest. "Mr. Jackson, it's good that you're here. I fear Mrs. Carlyle has lost her mind. She won't speak, and she won't come inside. I fear for her."

He swept past Maggie and took the stairs two at a time. He didn't bother to knock on Vivian's door, went straight through the room to the balcony, and stopped.

"I've been praying all night that he's still alive." Her voice was as limp as her raven hair hanging around her face.

It tore at his heart. "I'm sorry, Vivian."

"Me, too. For so many things. Life seems to be full of regrets. He was a good man. He deserved to live—not me."

He didn't like the sound of that comment. She was just as deserving of life as anyone else. "Vivian, let's go inside."

She turned her gaze on him. "I won't do it, Conner."

Won't come inside?

"I know that's what everyone is afraid of."

That comment didn't make sense. Was she talking about something else?

"I'm not planning to jump. I know that's what Maggie thinks I'll do."

Was she speaking the truth? He had no way of telling.

She took a step closer to him. "You believe me, don't you?"

He studied her, trying to discern the truth. "Let's go inside."

"Conner, it's important you believe me."

He wanted to, but he couldn't see past his heart. Any possible threat to her life, even from herself, was blurred by his love for her. "Prove it to me by coming inside."

She gave him a slight nod and walked back into her room. "Maggie, Conner and I will take tea in the parlor."

"You should go to bed, ma'am." Maggie shot him a worried look.

"Later. Mr. Jackson has come all this way to see that I am well. It would be improper to send him on his way without serving him tea." Vivian swept through the open doorway and headed down the stairs.

He gave Maggie a reassuring nod then followed after Vivian down to the parlor, where she stood at the window once again looking toward the water. He stood for several minutes, staring at her back, wondering what to say.

"I thought I knew what God wanted, but now it's all so unclear." Vivian's voice was soft. "Like a compass with its needle spinning round and round. I don't know what to do. I just wanted to be a good wife."

Maggie entered with the tea tray. He motioned for her to leave it, grateful to have a distraction. "Tea?"

Vivian turned quickly. "I'll serve."

He studied her as she poured him tea. Was she putting on a face of doing well? Or was it for his benefit so he would leave her be and she could do whatever was swirling around in her head?

"Sugar? Cream?"

"No, thank you." He took the dainty china cup she held out to him. *Lord, help me assess her mental state accurately.*

She prepared her own and took a sip. "I know you hold concern for me, but I will be fine."

Was she really fine?

"I survived the death of my first husband, and I will survive this, too." She stared straight into his eyes. "I promise you that I will do myself no harm."

He held her gaze. Could he believe her? He wanted to believe her. But more than believe in her, he wanted her to remain safe. He'd promised Randolph that he'd look after her while he was away, but what did that promise mean now? Was he still to look after her? Should he leave town? Should he stay? What was the *right* thing to do? It had all been so clear when Randolph was coming back and Conner would be leaving.

He, too, felt like a compass spinning without direction. *What do I do, Lord?*

❧

Conner woke two mornings later to his dog, Fred, standing on his chest, licking his face. Fred was a scruffy brown dog with a strong line of terrier in her. She'd ridded his previous employer's store of a rat problem in Seattle, and she'd kept Conner's store rat-free for the past two years. "I'm awake." He lifted Fred up into the air, but her tongue continued to lap in and out, trying to reach his face. He shifted her to one hand and lowered her to the floor before sitting and swinging his legs over the side of the bed.

The light coming in his window was brighter than it should be. What time was it? He plucked his pocket watch off the bedside table. Seven? He never slept that late. He put it up to his ear. The soft ticking of the inside works filtered into his ear.

Fred wiggled from the middle of her back down to the tip of her tail, shaking off whatever it was that dogs tried to get rid of.

"You have to go out, don't you, girl?" He pulled on his pants, swung on a shirt, and patted his leg. "Come on, girl." He headed downstairs and let Fred out the back door to the beach.

When he came back in with Fred, someone was banging furiously on his front door. Fred barked as she ran for the front of the store. He followed close behind. Scotty again. *Please, Lord, don't let anything have happened to Vivian.* He opened the door.

The old man huffed and puffed. "It's Mrs. Carlyle. She's gone."

Conner felt as though his rib cage were pressing in on his lungs. "What do you mean, gone? She didn't. . . ?"

Scotty shook his head. "We can't find her anywhere. Maggie searched the house three times. I searched the grounds and the stable. She's nowhere."

He raked his hands through his hair. "She can't have just disappeared. She has to be somewhere."

"Maggie says Mrs. Carlyle's red gown is gone and her black-hooded mantle."

"You head south and look on those streets, then head back to the house. I'll finish getting dressed, get my horse, then head north. I won't stop until I find her." He closed his door and rushed upstairs.

four

Vivian stared at the churning dark waters and the boiling sky. It wasn't so long ago that she'd enjoyed a storm like the one coming in, the storm that had likely killed her husband. If she'd known it had come from where Randolph was and had been a threat to him and his men, she would have viewed it differently. She had much to learn about ship travel and the dangers of the sea. What men might be out in this storm, scared? Terrified that they may never again see their loved ones. What wives, mothers, sisters, and daughters waited on the shore, hoping for their safe return?

Sailors milled around the dock. Most knew Randolph and respected her as his wife and left her alone. One seaman had approached her with ill will on his mind, but before she could pull out her Derringer, three sailors had threatened him and dragged him away with a warning never to go near her again. She heard slow, heavy footsteps approaching and slipped her hand into her pocket, wrapping her fingers around the pearl handle hidden there. The man stopped directly behind her. Should she pull out her Derringer and confront him? Or wait?

"Vivian," a man said in a hoarse whisper.

She turned to face Conner, anguish and relief etched on his face.

"What are you doing down here? Maggie's very worried about you."

"I didn't mean to worry anyone. I couldn't sleep. I want to say good-bye, but I don't know how."

"I know this is hard. A love like yours and Randolph's comes once in a lifetime."

A love like hers and Randolph's? She turned back to the water. How wrong outward impressions could be. In time, the ruse would have become reality. . .if Randolph had been able to forgive her. She sighed. "I didn't love him."

"What?"

She swung her gaze back to Conner. "I never loved him. Nor did he me. We married in haste. I was in need and took advantage of his attraction to me." Her looks had been a blessing as well as a curse. Had her first husband really loved her? Had any man? "I should have said no when he insisted we marry the day after we met, but I wanted the security of marriage. I was completely committed to Randolph. I was going to be the best wife I could for him, and I hoped to fall in love with him. There just wasn't time."

His silent stare unnerved her, so she went on, her voice thick with emotion. "Maybe if I hadn't married him until I was in love with him, he wouldn't have died. Maybe I shouldn't have married him at all. Maybe he would still be alive if he had never met me."

Conner took her shoulders in his hands. "Stop it. There was a freak accident. You had no control over the weather."

"But he might have been in a different place, and the lightning wouldn't have struck the ship." One small change might have made the difference.

"He was on the water. Lightning strikes the high point. Five miles this way or that, his ship still would have been the attraction for the bolts. It's not your fault."

He was right, but she wanted to blame herself. She looked back to the rolling water. "We fought the night he left."

"I know."

She jerked her gaze back to him.

"He had a few drinks and came to my store. That had been his habit when he was in port before he married you. In the three months you were married, he never once came, so I figured you must have fought. Why else would he come on his last night in port?"

She dipped her gaze away. "Did he tell you what we fought about?"

He shook his head. "I didn't think it was any of my business."

"What did he say?"

"He made me promise to look out for you while he was away."

Even after their fight, Randolph had been concerned for her well-being.

"Then I saw that he got to his ship."

Conner had always been there for her husband, and now he was here for her. He was a loyal and trustworthy friend. Randolph couldn't say enough good things about him. She'd felt like she'd known him before they ever met, and she wanted to rely on him now. Always. Her future was so uncertain. She'd been on a road for her life, and in marrying Randolph, she knew where it was going and what it would look like, even if Randolph threw her out. But now as the respectable widow of a favored captain, she didn't know what to do. Where to turn. Conner seemed like the only stable thing the Lord had placed in her life. She leaned into his chest.

He pushed her away after only a moment. "What are you doing?" His gaze darted around the dock. "There are sailors all around."

They wouldn't care. They'd probably cheer. "I'm sorry." An emptiness opened up inside her at his rebuff.

He looked up to the darkening sky. "Let's get you home."

She felt a raindrop land on her hand and let him lead her away.

❧

Conner lifted Vivian up onto Dakota's saddle sideways. The rain started coming harder, so he swung up behind her. "Hold on."

When she gripped the saddle horn instead of turning to

him, disappointment sank in his gut like lead. He goaded his horse into a trot. He shouldn't have pushed her away on the dock. He'd just been so shocked. The sailors wouldn't have minded, but she was the widow of a respected captain.

She never loved Randolph. He couldn't shake that thought. He would not do anything to tarnish her reputation nor Randolph's memory. It was still best if he left town, wasn't it? He didn't want to.

Dakota made short work of the trip and stopped in a puddle in front of Vivian's house. He nudged the horse forward to drier ground when Maggie flung open the door.

Maggie clutched her hands to her chest. "Thank the Lord you found her."

He swung down then lifted Vivian, carrying her up the steps and into the house. "She's fine."

Scotty pulled on his coat and hat. "I'll see to Dakota."

"Thank you, Scotty." He set Vivian down in the foyer. He didn't want to. He wanted to hold her. "Maggie, would you make Mrs. Carlyle some tea? I'm sure she's cold."

"The water's hot. It'll only take a moment." Maggie hastened away.

He took Vivian's cape then guided her into the parlor and near the fireplace. "I'll build this up nice and warm for you."

Vivian didn't move as he worked, and soon Maggie came in and gave them both a cup of hot tea. "Mercy me, we have to get you out of that dress and into something proper."

"I'm fine, Maggie." Vivian's voice was soft, almost shy. "My dress isn't even wet."

"It's red! You should be wearing black. I took the liberty of dyeing that orange dress you never liked. It should be dry. We'll put that on you until we can have some proper mourning clothes made for you."

"Very well, I'll change later. But I won't have any other black dresses made. One will be sufficient. Is that clear? I'll not waste the money."

Maggie nodded.

Vivian waved a hand. "You may go."

Maggie dipped her head and turned to leave.

"And, Maggie, thank you."

Maggie beamed and left.

Conner took a swallow of his tea. "Is the fire all right?"

"It's lovely, but you're soaked."

"I'm not so bad. My coat in the foyer took most of it." He set his tea on the mantel. "Out on the dock, when I pushed you away—"

"Please, Conner, don't. I was overcome and wanted a little comfort. I shouldn't have imposed. I'm fine now."

"I know you said you weren't in love with Randolph, but you're still grieving a loss. He was my friend, too." He held his hands from his side. "I could use a little comfort, too."

"Oh, Conner, I never thought about how this was your loss, as well." She stepped to him.

He wrapped his arms around her. He wanted to hold her forever. Just because he was in love with her didn't mean she would ever have feelings for him. He wanted to kiss her but stepped away before he felt the embrace had crossed the line of impropriety. Maybe it already had. His friend was barely dead, and he was thinking about kissing his widow. What kind of man was he? He should give up on Vivian while he still could and leave town as planned.

She studied him a moment like he was a new face to her. "Do you remember what I said the other day about the compass?"

He nodded. "You felt like you were the needle spinning around."

She took a sip of tea. "Do you know that a ballerina fixes her gaze on a stationary object as she twirls around and around? When she stops, she's not dizzy because she kept her eyes fixed on one thing. I'm trying to keep fixed on the Lord and know that He will take care of me. I don't feel so dizzy.

But when I look at you, I don't feel dizzy, either. The Lord and you are both stationary objects for me. He in heaven, and you in the flesh."

He wasn't sure how to feel about that.

"I don't mean to occupy all your time or take you away from your duties or your store. But for now, until the Lord helps me figure things out, if I can look to you, I know I won't get so dizzy I fall down."

"I don't know what to say."

"I believe He has placed you in my path to help me through all this. I promise not to be a burden to you, but if you'd rather not. . ."

"You could never be a burden. I'm glad to help in any way I can."

"Thank you. You always were a good friend to Randolph."

Not as good as she might think or he wouldn't have had feelings for her. "Have you thought about a service for Randolph?"

She sucked in a breath. "But there is no body to bury."

"Men are lost at sea all the time, bodies rarely recovered." He couldn't tell her that whatever was left after the explosion was probably eaten by a shark or other sea creature. "It'll give you closure."

Her brow furrowed. "It would be the proper thing to do, wouldn't it?"

He nodded.

"What do I need to do?"

"I'll talk to Minister Sciuto and make all the arrangements. You don't have to worry about anything." He wanted to take care of everything for her. Take care of her, too.

He left shortly after that to the clouds' steady offering of rain. How could he leave town now after promising Vivian to be her anchor through this? *Lord, I guess I'm staying if that's what You want. Please help me show proper decorum and not dishonor You, Vivian, or Randolph's memory.*

After Conner left, Vivian stood in her room and inhaled as Maggie cinched her corset a wee bit tighter to fit her into her mourning dress. The dress wasn't nearly so bad in black as it had been in peach. Any orangey colors made her look as though she was recovering from a long illness.

"You must've gained a little weight since the captain commissioned this dress for you." Maggie huffed with exertion behind her.

"It's all your fine cooking. You spoil me."

Maggie held out the bodice. "It might not be the fixin's."

Vivian slipped her arms into the sleeves. "What's that supposed to mean?"

Maggie stepped behind her and started hooking up the back. "You've been married three months. You could be carrying a little one."

The breath froze inside her lungs, and she put a hand on her belly. Did she want to have a baby, Randolph's baby? It would be a fitting tribute to him, but she knew he wouldn't want her to be the mother of his only heir. *Lord, Your will be done in this. If I am to be the mother of Randolph's child, let it be a son. He would have liked that. And help me to train him up to be an honorable man who follows closely after You.*

"All done." Maggie nodded at her. "Now you look the proper widow and very becoming in black."

She gazed at her reflection. "But black is so dreary. Do you know that in Mississippi the governor tried to pass a law banning mourning clothes after the War Between the States? Everyone had lost someone, and it was depressing to have the whole state in black."

"Now we aren't in Mississippi, are we? We're in Washington State. And that war was over long before you were born."

Randolph hadn't had the wife he wanted, but maybe she could be the kind of widow he would have been proud of. "Maggie, what do we have to fill my basket?"

"You aren't going to feed the birds? Today?"

"It stopped raining. They have to eat. They were expecting me yesterday."

Maggie took a deep breath. "I'll have Scotty hitch up the carriage."

She opened her mouth to protest, but Maggie held up her hand and went on quickly. "I don't want no fuss from you. You're a widow now, and I won't have you walking around when you are in black."

She opened her mouth to object.

"One word of fuss from you and I'll have Scotty bolt this door shut. I'll talk to Scotty and meet you in the kitchen."

"Maggie."

The housekeeper turned in the doorway with a look of determination. She was a feisty woman, and she was just trying to look after her mistress.

"Thank you."

Vivian had the basket half full by the time Maggie entered the kitchen.

"The carriage will be around front in a jiffy." Maggie walked into the pantry and came out with a paper sack. "I was so upset yesterday that I had to bake. I think those birds will like these gingersnaps."

"You're a peach." She put them into her basket, and she walked out front with Maggie as Scotty drove up in the carriage. Scotty helped her into the carriage then assisted Maggie with her own basket for shopping.

Maggie insisted that she be dropped off at the fish market first, and Scotty stayed with Vivian. She didn't object because she knew that Maggie would win. She left Scotty in the carriage and went down to the beach. She barely sat when Peter came running with the others close behind.

"Where were you yesterday? We couldn't find you." Peter jumped up onto the log next to her.

"I'm sorry I couldn't make it." She didn't want to explain her troubles to them. They had enough of their own. "Let's thank the Lord for this food."

They joined hands and all said, "Thank You, Jesus, for this food. Amen."

She handed out the food. "How is that other loose tooth of yours?"

Peter bared his teeth, or at least what was left of them, then fished in his pocket, pulling out a white baby tooth.

She smiled. "It came out."

"He kept pulling at it until it came out," Tommy said, looking half jealous that Peter would be getting another penny. "There was blood all over his face."

"Can I have another penny?"

Betsy looked up. "That's not polite. You don't ask people for money."

"But she gave me one last time."

She had forgotten the pennies. "I haven't any. I'll bring you one next time. One for each of you."

Peter wiped his mouth with his sleeve. "Why're you wearing black?"

"Peter! That's not nice." Betsy piped up.

"Well, I don't like black. It makes me sad."

It made her sad, too, but out of respect for Randolph she was almost glad she was wearing it.

Betsy put her hand on Peter's arm. "It means she knows someone who died."

Peter looked at Vivian with big brown eyes. Eyes that could melt any girl's heart. "Who died?"

Betsy huffed and shook her head.

"It's all right, Betsy." There was no reason not to tell them. "Have you ever heard of Captain Carlyle?"

They all shook their heads except George. "He's your husband, and a mighty fine captain, from what I hear."

"That's right, but his ship sank."

"Did he swim to shore?" Peter's eyes rounded even more.

She wrapped her arm around the boy. "No. He didn't."

"He's the one who died, silly," Betsy said.

Peter sat up straighter and frowned. "He shouldn't have died. Didn't he know you would be sad for him?"

She hugged Peter. His simple comment warmed her heart. "He didn't have a choice. He was on his ship when it got struck by lightning."

When Betsy had eaten part of her food and put the rest in her pocket, Vivian took out the yard goods scraps, needle, and thread. "First, I'll show you how to thread a needle and sew two pieces of fabric together." If Betsy could learn simple sewing skills, maybe she could apprentice with a real seamstress and not live her life on the streets or in some seedy back room.

&

Vivian was tired by the time she returned from visiting the children. She stared up at the two-story blue Victorian house. She didn't feel as though she belonged here, but where else should she go? Wasn't the house hers now? She entered and walked around, slowly surveying everything in it. Nothing of hers was there. It was all Randolph. He wouldn't like for her to start changing things, but she didn't feel comfortable here knowing Randolph disapproved of her. Would he want her out of his house?

A throat cleared behind her. "Ma'am."

"Yes, Maggie."

Maggie looked a bit nervous but squared her shoulders. "I know you said not to, but there will be a seamstress arriving momentarily to measure you for a new mourning dress."

She thinned her lips. Just because she had money didn't mean she should waste it. "You have wasted her time then because I'm not commissioning another mourning dress. This one will do fine, and if I need another, we can dye one of the many other dresses Randolph bought me." Randolph had spared no expense on her wardrobe.

"She's a widow."

She relaxed her mouth.

"She has a small son to provide for."

Maggie knew just how to pull at her heartstrings. "Is she bad off?"

"She's going to lose her home soon."

"When will she arrive?"

Maggie went to the window. "I think that's her walking up the street."

"Hurry. Help me get out of this dress." She headed for the stairs.

Maggie trailed after her. "Why?"

"I'll wear the gray dress or another one. If I'm wearing black, she might think I don't really need a mourning dress."

"You're a wealthy woman. You don't need a reason to purchase another dress."

"Just help me out of this." She knew that this woman would want meaningful work and not just charity handouts.

Maggie unhooked the back of the bodice. The doorbell chimed.

"Put her in the parlor and then come back up to help me."

As Maggie hurried from the room, Vivian shucked out of the rest of the dress. She got her gray dress and had the skirt on and fastened and the bodice pulled on when Maggie returned.

"She's in the parlor. I served her tea and gingersnaps. Her son is a little cutie. He'll steal your heart."

She put her hand on her stomach as Maggie hooked up the back of her bodice. Would she be having a son?

She wanted to rush down the stairs and greet this poor widow, but she took the stairs slowly and entered the parlor to see a sunny-faced woman smiling at her four-year-old son.

Maggie cleared her throat. "Mrs. Parker, this is Mrs. Carlyle."

The woman stood, straightening her blue dress and schooling her smile. "I'm sorry, ma'am." She put her hand on her son's shoulder. "Harry won't be any trouble, I promise. He's a good boy." The poor woman looked so nervous.

Vivian smiled at the blond woman. "It's no problem. Please sit." Mrs. Parker didn't look like a widow. She hadn't really expected the woman to be dressed in black, but without it, she looked like any other woman. How long a widow? How long would she herself be required to wear mourning garb?

She turned to the boy and held out the plate of gingersnaps. "Would you like a cookie?"

The boy looked up at her with big brown eyes. When he nodded his head, his blond curls danced. He reminded her of Peter with blond hair. He didn't take a cookie; instead, he looked to his mother, who nodded. Mrs. Parker held up one finger, and he reached out a chubby hand and took just one.

"What do you say, Harry?" Mrs. Parker prodded.

The cookie hovered between his lips, but he managed to say, "Thank you."

Mrs. Parker turned her blue eyes on her. "Thank you, Mrs. Carlyle, for the cookie as well as the opportunity to interview with you. I wore my best dress so you could see my sewing. I also made Harry's clothes." She held out her arm for Vivian to inspect her work.

"Please call me Vivian." She made a show of studying the dress, then looking at Harry's clothes. She wanted the woman to think she'd given it thought and wasn't just handing out charity. Some people were proud. *But if you got hungry enough, or your son got hungry enough, even a proud person would stoop to accepting charity. . .and even lower.*

"Please call me Abigail." Abigail handed her a small patch-work of fabrics. "I brought this so you could see my stitches."

The stitching was even and smooth, better than Vivian had ever done. "Abigail, as you can see, I'm in need of a mourning dress, and rather quickly so. How soon would you be able to complete it?"

"If I work very hard, a week."

"Fine. I'll have Scotty bring round the carriage while you take my measurements, and we can go choose a pattern and fabric right now, if that suits you?"

Abigail smiled. "The sooner I have all the materials, the sooner I can have your dress completed."

Vivian took Abigail and Harry to an uptown shop, purchased everything needed to make the dress, and dropped them off at their little house with a FOR SALE sign in the front yard. It warmed her inside to know she was helping a woman in need. A side benefit was that Maggie wouldn't harp on her for only having one appropriate mourning dress.

When she returned home, Maggie met her at the front door and handed her an envelope. "This came by special messenger."

She turned it over. Benton, Attorney at Law. Randolph's lawyer. She broke the seal.

"Mr. Jackson is waiting for you in the back garden."

What was Conner doing here in the middle of the day? It must be important. He had a store to run. She thanked Maggie and went out back. Conner stood in the yard by her lilac bushes, whose leaves were beginning to turn color. "Conner, is everything all right?"

He turned and met her on the stone patio. "How are you doing?"

"You left your store and came here in the middle of the day to ask me how I am?" But then why shouldn't he? Scotty had been at his store first thing two mornings on her behalf. "I'm fine."

Maggie came out and set a tea tray on the patio table. "Shall I serve?"

"I'll do it. Thank you, Maggie." She sat at the table, setting her envelope down, and gave Conner a cup of tea.

"Thank you." Conner took a sip, then set his cup down before reaching into his coat pocket and pulling out an envelope similar to hers. "I came about this. I'll come and get you and take you. You shouldn't have to go alone."

She picked up her envelope. "I just received one, too. I haven't read it yet. Maggie told me you were waiting for me. What does it say?"

"It's about Randolph's will."

Her breath stilled in her chest for a moment before she could breathe again. "I hadn't thought about a will."

"I'm sure he left you everything."

If Randolph had had time before he sailed, he wouldn't have left her anything. "Then why would you have received a notice?"

He looked at her, concerned for a moment. "We're old friends."

She hoped Randolph did leave Conner something of value. He'd always been a good friend to her husband. He deserved something for his friendship and loyalty all these years. "I would appreciate the company."

"The reading is in three days, the day after the funeral, at two. I'll come for you at one thirty." He stood, gave her a small bow, and left.

She put her hand on her belly. If a baby was growing inside her, it would be good to know what Randolph had left his child. She opened the envelope and read it briefly. She was to be at the attorney's office at one thirty, not two. It also said that if that was inconvenient or she would prefer he come to the house, he would make those arrangements.

She went into the parlor and sat at the writing desk. She penned one letter to the attorney saying she would be at his office at one thirty in three days and penned a second informing Conner she would meet him at the attorney's. Then she sent Scotty to deliver them. Conner came that evening to tell her he would arrive at one and still accompany her; then he stayed for supper.

five

Two days later, Vivian sat in the front pew of the church with a multitude of Randolph's mourners gathered behind her. Most of them likely attended as a social obligation. She wished all but his true friends had stayed home; that would be the best way to honor the dead.

She turned her focus to the wreath of fall flowers with a sash of black crepe. All that there was to represent a life. How sad. *I'm sorry it wasn't me, Randolph. You were a good man, better than me. I might be carrying your son. I'll raise him well and tell him all about his brave sea captain father.*

She was as much a hypocrite as some of the others in attendance. A tear trickled down her cheek. She went to wipe it away with her gloved hand when a black handkerchief dangled in front of her. She took it and looked up at Conner. "Thank you." She dabbed at her face.

He stood tall and lean and was quite handsome in his black suit. "It'll be starting soon." He sat next to her.

Maggie and Scotty sat at the other end of her pew. They were going to sit in the back, but she insisted that they sit up front with her. She didn't want to sit alone, and they were as close to Randolph as she—probably closer. They had known him longer, and Randolph always regarded them highly. She'd appreciated that Randolph treated them well and spoke to them with respect, from one human being to another.

Minister Sciuto's words about her husband were beautiful. Then Conner stood up front and shared about his childhood friend.

"I met Randolph twenty years ago. He was ten and I was seven and his brother, William, was five. At a time in my life when the whole human race looked hopeless to me, I admired and respected Randolph. He always looked out for me and William. He was a friend and claimed me as a brother."

Vivian choked up. In her own troubles, she'd forgotten just how close Conner had been to her husband all his life. He must be grieving terribly. It was a far greater loss for him than it was for her, and that saddened her further. She cried for Conner's loss. Conner ended by reading a lengthy poem called *The Rime of the Ancient Mariner*, Randolph's favorite. Since she'd become a Christian, she'd been plagued with the question of God really loving her with her past. So when Randolph had recited this poem for her, she'd latched on to the third stanza from the end. Now she listened for it:

> *He prayeth best, who loveth best*
> *All things both great and small;*
> *For the dear God who loveth us,*
> *He made and loveth all.*

It once again comforted her to know that God made her and that He loved her in spite of herself.

When Conner finished, he sat back down next to her. She gripped his hand to comfort him. He squeezed back. The remainder of the service, she sat with her hand in his, afraid to take the comfort from him; he'd suffered such a deep loss.

At the conclusion of the service, she was ushered out a side door to a waiting carriage. The carriage she shared with Conner came immediately after the minister's carriage. There were no pallbearers to keep him company, and there was no hearse between that carriage and hers. There was no need. There was no body. It bothered her that she couldn't put Randolph's body to rest in the ground. But he was a seaman through and through and probably preferred to die at sea rather than on land.

She stood beside an empty grave. Not even a grave. A stone

marker to remember the passing of a life. Conner had had an image of Randolph's ship engraved in the stone:

> *Captain Randolph Carlyle*
> *Devoted Husband*
> *May he rest at peace in God's loving arms*
> *March 1, 1868–September 29, 1898*

Devoted husband. Conner had suggested putting *loving husband* on the marker, but Vivian knew that wouldn't be accurate. Loathing had filled Randolph's eyes the night he left. Yet she could concede that he might·have been devoted to her, at least for a time. If she could only go back and change it all. She knew he wanted to marry her because of her beauty, and she wanted the security of marriage. She would never make that mistake again. She would only marry for love. Someone who could love her in spite of her past.

She gripped the white roses in her hands. Maggie had cut them from Randolph's own garden and lovingly removed all the thorns for her. A last remembrance of a man who loved the sea and loved his roses. If he could have taken his rosebushes on the ship with him, he would have had no reason to step foot on land.

Minister Sciuto began speaking: "Randolph John Carlyle. Captain. Husband. Friend."

The minister's voice faded away as she lowered her head. Tears gathered in her eyes but not for the reason that other widows had tears at their husband's funeral. So many regrets.

six

The day following the funeral, Maggie helped Vivian into her dyed mourning dress once again. She wasn't with child. She knew that now. Her time had come. She had been looking forward to the challenge of motherhood and raising Randolph's son to be an honorable man that Randolph would have been proud to call his son. It would have given her a purpose. . .direction and somehow redeemed her. Now all she had was herself.

Conner rode up on Dakota, and Scotty had the carriage waiting out front. Conner gave Dakota's reins to Scotty and took the carriage with Vivian. They arrived at the attorney's office just before one thirty and were ushered into his office precisely at the appointed time.

Mr. Benton was a plump man in his sixties with a welcoming smile. "Please sit down." After Vivian had taken a seat, Conner and Mr. Benton also sat down. Mr. Benton looked over his glasses from her to Conner. "Mr. Jackson, I was not expecting you until two."

Conner nodded. "I didn't want Mrs. Carlyle to have to face any of this alone."

Mr. Benton shuffled some papers. "This puts me in a bit of an awkward position. I have a private matter I wish to speak about to Mrs. Carlyle before I read the terms of the will."

Conner stood immediately. "I'll wait in the reception area."

Mr. Benton stood as well. "Thank you. We won't be long."

Her stomach knotted. She'd wanted Conner here with her, but what if the attorney knew something of her past. She didn't want that revealed to Conner. Mr. Benton had said a private matter.

When the door closed behind Conner, the lawyer sat back down behind his mahogany desk and smiled at her. "There is a matter concerning your husband's will."

Her insides twisted tighter. "What is it?"

"Captain Carlyle came to me about changing his will."

When had he had time after their fight?

"He'd said he'd been lax in making arrangements since marrying. His intent was to add you to his will. I prepared the document, but he hadn't come in yet to sign it."

"I don't understand."

"You are not mentioned in your husband's legal will."

She would get nothing. Had a part of Randolph known she hadn't been honest with him and was that why he'd put off changing his will? "Then there's no need for me to be here."

"On the contrary. I have his revised will that includes you."

"But it's not signed and therefore not legal." She still got nothing. That's how Randolph would have wanted it in the end. Her just reward.

"And that's why I didn't want Mr. Jackson in here. We can petition the court to consider this new will, though unsigned. I will testify on your behalf and inform the court of Captain Carlyle's intent. If the other parties listed in your husband's will don't object, you should get your share."

"And if they do?"

"We might be able to get you something. You were, after all, Captain Carlyle's legal wife. I was your husband's attorney, and now I'll be yours."

She studied the man. "Mr. Jackson is in my husband's will, isn't he? That's why you've summoned him."

Mr. Benton nodded. "And why I didn't want him present during this meeting with you. If you choose to pursue this, we would be petitioning against Mr. Conner Jackson and Mr. William Carlyle."

She'd kept a secret from Randolph that she knew he wouldn't have approved of, ever. William had warned her.

When Randolph returned, he wouldn't have signed the new will that included her. A will was to carry out a person's wishes, and she was sure that Randolph's wishes didn't include leaving her anything. "Leave his will as it is. We weren't married very long. Mr. Jackson and Randolph's brother are more deserving."

"Mrs. Carlyle, please reconsider. The length of time you were married has no bearing on whether or not you're deserving."

No, but her secret was. She'd married Randolph with a lie between them that she knew he would never accept. She didn't deserve any of Randolph's money or possessions. "I've made up my mind."

Mr. Benton shook his head. "I'll give you a week to reconsider the ramifications of your actions, and then we'll talk again on this matter. I would be doing Randolph a disservice if I didn't at least try to persuade you to take action."

If he knew what she knew about how Randolph felt about her past, he wouldn't insist, so she simply nodded. "I'll wait out in the lobby while you speak with Mr. Jackson."

≈

Conner stood when he saw Vivian exit Mr. Benton's office. She looked neither unduly upset nor pleased. What had Randolph left her?

"Mr. Jackson, won't you come in?"

"What about Mrs. Carlyle?"

"I'll wait out here."

"Why?" He looked from her to the attorney and back.

"The reading is just for you."

He turned back to Mr. Benton. "Shouldn't she be there for the reading?"

"There are extenuating circumstances that don't require Mrs. Carlyle to be present." Mr. Benton motioned for Conner to enter his office.

This was all very odd. "Can Mrs. Carlyle be present if I want her to be?"

Mr. Benton nodded.

He turned to Vivian and held out his hand to her. "Please come."

She glanced at Mr. Benton then took Conner's hand. Why had she hesitated?

When Mr. Benton finished reading the will, Conner stared at the man. There had to be more. There had to be something for Vivian. William inherited the house and half of Carlyle Shipping, and he'd inherited the other half of the shipping enterprise. What was left for Vivian? "There has to be more. What about Mrs. Carlyle?"

"As I explained to Mrs. Carlyle, Captain Carlyle hadn't signed his new will that named her as a beneficiary. The will he had in place before he married is legal and binding."

"But she should get something. She was his wife."

"I'm not going to pursue it," Vivian said.

"Pursue what?"

Mr. Benton took a deep breath. "I have counseled Mrs. Carlyle to petition the courts to consider the intent of Captain Carlyle's new will that he had not yet signed."

"Then do it. What will she get?"

"Half the house and one third of the shipping business. It's in your best interest to find yourself an attorney."

Mr. Benton had no idea what was in Conner's best interest. "I won't fight." Vivian's well-being was in his best interest.

"It's okay. I'll write to William, and as soon as he can come and take possession of the house, I'll leave."

His gut clenched. She couldn't leave. He wouldn't let her. "This is wrong."

She turned soulful eyes on him. "This is the way Randolph left his affairs. I will honor that."

Why? He wanted to fight for her. "Randolph would want you taken care of. He asked me to see that you were taken care of if anything should happen to him." Had Randolph sensed something? "I made a promise."

"Please let it be."

He didn't want to, but because she asked, he would. . . for now.

On the carriage ride back to her house, she said, "I'll write to William and ask him what he'd like to do about the house. Maybe he and Sarah will move up here. I think they'd like it here, don't you?"

What did it matter if William and his wife would like it here? "I'll write to William, as well, and tell him Randolph died before he could change his will. I know he will insist on honoring the new will, even unsigned."

"Don't. I won't accept it. Promise me you won't ask anything of William on my behalf."

"Why not?"

"I have my reasons. Please, Conner."

He couldn't refuse her and nodded, but he could still tell William what he thought without asking anything of him. William was an honorable man like Randolph; he would do the right thing. And from what Conner understood, William's wife was a friend of Vivian's. Certainly she wouldn't stop William from doing what was right and fair.

"Would you like to come inside, or do you need to get back to your store?"

If he stayed, he'd probably just make her mad trying to convince her to take action. "I should get back. Martin might be overwhelmed." He should head over to Randolph's shipping business and see what state his affairs were in.

ช

Vivian entered her foyer, and Maggie took her cape. "Mrs. Parker and her son are in the parlor."

When Vivian strode through the doorway, Abigail was once again smiling at her son. An emptiness opened in her belly; she wouldn't be having a son.

"Abigail, it's so good to see you again."

Abigail turned, her gaze flickered down Vivian's dress, and her smile dipped slightly. "I wanted to fit the bodice on you and size the waist of the skirt."

Vivian looked down at the dress she had on, her black mourning dress. Should she say something about it or let it pass? Abigail had obviously noticed. "I'm sure you are wondering about my dress."

"Your wardrobe is none of my concern, except for the dress you have commissioned from me."

She sat. "I'll tell you anyway. This was a dress I already owned that I never liked. It was peach, which is a dreadful color on me. Maggie dyed it so I would have something appropriate to wear until I could have a dress made. It's better in black, but I still don't like it much. I've never been fond of black."

"Sad," Harry said from his seat next to his mother.

Abigail patted her son's leg. "That's right." Then she turned to Vivian. "Harry thinks black is sad and refused to wear it after a time."

"If you don't mind my asking, how long did you wear mourning clothes?"

"Three months to the day. It was as if something inside Harry said enough mourning. It's time to get on with living. I still grieve my loss, but I try to be happy as much as I can in front of Harry."

"How long since your husband passed away?"

"Six months next week." Tears welled in Abigail's eyes. "We've almost run out of the money my husband saved. I don't know where we will go when we lose the house."

"You're young. You'll find another husband."

"I hope not. I don't know if I could handle another loss." A tear slipped down Abigail's cheek. She quickly swiped it away and stole a glance at her son. Harry hadn't noticed as he was busy picking cookie crumbs off his jacket.

An ache welled up inside Vivian to have a love like that. She hadn't had that with her first husband and certainly not with Randolph.

After Abigail left, she prayed for Abigail and her small son. She also prayed to find a love like the one Abigail had had with her husband. Then she sat down and wrote a letter to William, telling him about Randolph's death, what he'd been left in the will, and asking him what he wanted her to do about his newly inherited house. After that, she went to bed without supper. It had been a long day, and she was exhausted. Tomorrow she would consider what she was to do with the rest of her life.

seven

Conner entered Carlyle Shipping. The sandy-haired clerk was leaning back in his chair with his feet up on his desk, eyes closed.

Conner cleared his throat.

The man looked up at him with sleepy eyes, then suddenly came alert, dropping his feet to the floor. "What can I do for you, sir?"

"I want to talk to whomever is in charge here."

"Captain Carlyle owns Carlyle Shipping, but Mr. Abernathy manages the office."

"Are you aware that Captain Carlyle recently died?"

The man sat straighter and swallowed hard. "Yes, sir. We've been running things as usual. Mr. Abernathy says he still has a business to run, orders and shipping to provide and schedule."

"It sounds like Mr. Abernathy thinks he's inherited the captain's business."

"I don't know, sir. I'm just a clerk."

"What's your name?"

"Jonathan Kirkide, sir."

"Please stop calling me sir. My name is Conner Jackson, and I'm one of the new owners of Carlyle Shipping."

The young man's eyes grew wide. "Yes, sir, Mr. Jackson, sir. Oops. Sorry, sir. I mean, Mr. Jackson."

He wasn't going to discuss the future of Carlyle Shipping with a clerk. "I need to see Mr. Abernathy now."

"Yes, sir." Jonathan stood so fast that his chair tipped back to the wall behind him. "Right this way." Jonathan guided him down a hallway and through a door to the warehouse where men were busy moving crates.

Conner followed Jonathan up a flight of stairs to an office that overlooked the warehouse floor.

Jonathan knocked on, then opened the door. "Mr. Abernathy, Mr. Jackson to see you."

Mr. Abernathy, a middle-aged man with a handlebar mustache, sat at ease behind the large mahogany desk. "I'm busy right now. Make an appointment with Mr. Kirkide, and I'll see you later in the week."

Conner stepped into the room and up to the desk. "Mr. Abernathy, let me introduce myself, Conner Jackson, one of the new owners of Carlyle Shipping."

Mr. Abernathy's gaze shifted up but his head did not move. "Is that so?"

Conner reached into his inside coat pocket and pulled out a letter. "This is from Captain Carlyle's attorney."

Mr. Abernathy made a point of reading the letter carefully and slowly before refolding it and handing it back. Then he stood and held out his hand. "It's good to meet you. Please have a seat."

There was something in the hardness of the man's face that belied his pleasant-sounding words. Conner shook the man's hand and sat.

Mr. Abernathy steepled his fingers. "We all speculated that the captain's new wife would get the business. Of course I planned to run the business as usual for her. No need to worry the poor widow with business affairs."

Conner didn't like the slightly demeaning tone in the manager's voice. "There is some dispute as to Mrs. Carlyle's portion of the business, but I'm taking charge until the other owners and I, along with the attorneys, can decide just how to distribute this asset. Until then, I'll be making all decisions."

Mr. Abernathy's eyes narrowed ever so slightly. If he hadn't been looking, Conner would have missed it. "Of course. I'm at your service. The captain trusted me with all aspects of this business, so I can answer any questions you have."

"What is the state of the business?"

"Business has not been so good lately, but we're in the black, barely."

He didn't like Mr. Abernathy speaking of Randolph's business with so much possessiveness. "I would like to see the account books if you don't mind."

"Why should I mind? You're part owner now." Mr. Abernathy stood a little too eagerly. "Right this way." He walked through a door at the side of his office into an adjoining office where a brunette woman in her thirties sat behind the desk.

"Miss Demarco, this is Mr. Jackson, one of the new owners."

Her eyes widened slightly. "Is that so?" She gave him a tip of her head. "It's nice to meet you."

Conner noted a bit of insincerity in her greeting.

"Mr. Jackson would like to see the books."

"I can assure you they're all in order."

He hoped they were. "I appreciate you keeping the books so well. If I can just look through them to get an overall view of Carlyle Shipping so I can let the other owners know how the business is fairing. . ."

Miss Demarco seemed reluctant to give up her books but finally said, "Certainly. How far back would you like to go?"

"Let me start with the most recent and go back a year to start."

Miss Demarco pulled several ledger books and placed them on her well-ordered desk. "I'll finish recording today's totals in the morning, if that is all right with you, Mr. Abernathy?"

"That will be fine. Come to my office. I have some other work for you."

Conner determined to be at this office more often than Randolph would have had time for. The people here had an air about them that this was their company and not Randolph's. He poured over the books for three hours until he was starting to see cross-eyed.

Conner's head was pounding by the time he left the shipping office. It would be a sweet relief to see Vivian.

First, he stopped by his store. It was late. Martin should have closed up by now. The CLOSED sign was in place and the door locked. He unlocked and opened the door to find Martin sitting on a stool behind the counter looking guilty with an open can of beans in his hand and his mouth full. He chewed quickly and swallowed. "I was really hungry."

Martin deserved more than a measly can of beans for all he did. He waved the younger man off. "Why haven't you gone home?" Fred trotted over and stood on her haunches. He picked her up.

Martin dropped his spoon into the can. "I wasn't sure what to do when you didn't come back from the attorney's. I knew you'd be back eventually and thought I should wait. . .but I got hungry." Martin dipped his head as though guilty of some great crime.

Martin was young, only twenty-three, but he was reliable. Conner couldn't say that about his other transient employees. Now he understood how Ian, his own former boss, had felt about him. Conner had just done his job as well as he could, always a fear in the back of his mind that Ian would terminate his employ or find someone else to do his job better. But now that he had employees of his own, he understood the value of reliable help. He grabbed a bag of Saratoga chips and tossed them to Martin. "Enjoy, and don't worry about the beans." He would have to reward Martin in some other way, as well. With so many dishonorable people around, Martin needed to know that he was appreciated. "Go home. I'll see you tomorrow."

Martin swung on his coat and grabbed the bag of chips.

As Martin opened the door and prepared to step outside, Conner said, "Thanks."

Martin shot him a smile and a nod then was gone into the night.

Conner looked at his pocket watch. Vivian would be sitting

down to supper any minute. If he hurried, he might garner an invitation to join her. He locked up the shop and rode Dakota at a gallop uptown.

The black crepe on Vivian's door weighed heavy on him. He wished Randolph were coming back, but at the same time, there was Vivian. He was being torn apart by this conflict and didn't know how to resolve it. He could still leave town.

He knocked softly. Maggie opened the door to let him in. "Good evening, Mr. Jackson."

He smiled at the plump older woman. "I wish you'd call me Conner."

"You know I can't do that."

He nodded. "Is Mrs. Carlyle in the dining room?" He hoped she hadn't eaten early and he was too late.

"She went to bed an hour ago and fell right asleep."

"It's only suppertime. She can't be sleeping." Conner couldn't believe it. Something had to be wrong.

"She was very tired from the day." Maggie tried to placate him. "She will feel better tomorrow."

"I want to see her."

Maggie squared her shoulders. "I'm sorry, Mr. Jackson. You'll have to come back tomorrow."

"I need to know she's all right."

"She was fine when she went to bed."

"That was an hour ago. Please go check on her for me."

Maggie seemed reluctant but finally conceded. "You wait here." She headed up the stairs one slow step at a time.

When she was halfway up, a scream came from above. He took the stairs three at a time, overtaking Maggie quickly, who sped up. He burst through Vivian's door and stared at her thrashing the covers around with her hands and feet.

Maggie hurried past him. "Just a bad dream." She braced her hands on his chest and pushed him out into the hall. "You stay out here." She went to Vivian's side and soothed her with a gentle hand on her forehead, apparently without waking her.

Vivian calmed, and Maggie smoothed the covers back into place before returning to the hall and closing the door. "The past week has been very hard on her. She hasn't slept well."

It had been a long week, and Conner hadn't had the comfort of a good night's sleep, either. He went home to bed and flopped most of the night like a dying fish cast upon the shore.

eight

Conner sat in the chair opposite Mr. Benton. "Do you have the papers for me to sign?"

"Are you sure you want to do this? Even if Mrs. Carlyle chooses to petition the courts, it doesn't mean she will win."

"Randolph was my best friend. I would be dishonoring him to cheat his widow. Before Randolph left, he asked me to take care of Mrs. Carlyle should anything happen to him."

Mr. Benton opened a folder. "This document turns over one quarter of Carlyle Shipping to Mrs. Carlyle, half of what you inherited. That is very generous of you."

"I have my own business that is doing well. I don't need half of Carlyle Shipping." He didn't need any of it. The gold rush had been a huge boon to his business with miners pouring through town to head north to Alaska. He was wealthier than he ever thought he would be. But his gift to Vivian wasn't all that unselfish. As long as both he and she were part owners, she would be a part of his life. That's the way he wanted it. If he stayed close to her during her time of mourning, he'd be aware if any other man began to show an interest in her before he could tell her his feelings and court her. No, he wasn't being generous; he was being cautious and looking out for his own interests.

He took the pen and dipped it into the inkwell. Satisfaction wrapped around his heart as he scratched his name on the line, binding his life with Vivian's.

Mr. Benton blotted the signature and blew on it before setting it aside. "These next documents give me the right to transfer funds from Carlyle Shipping to a new account in Mrs. Carlyle's name."

"She doesn't have to know I set this up, does she?"

Mr. Benton shook his head. "She's coming in to my office in two days. I'll suggest that it must have been Captain Carlyle."

"It'll be six months worth of her share of the profits from Carlyle shipping?" He didn't want her to get suspicious with regular deposits. It would put him in a bit of a pinch, but he figured he'd be all right.

"I don't think the business can handle that amount all at once. I'll have just part of one month's profits to start with put into the account. That should be plenty for her needs. I'll talk to the banker, so when I take Mrs. Carlyle to the bank to sign over the account to her, he will tell her that arrangements have been made for a monthly allotment to be deposited into her personal account from Carlyle Shipping." Mr. Benton turned the document to face him. "If those terms suit you, sign all three pages."

As long as Vivian thought Randolph had set this up and she would have money enough, that was all he was concerned with. He scratched his name on all the lines.

"Now if you will accompany me to the bank, we'll get the account set up in her name."

&

On Thursday, Vivian sat in Mr. Benton's reception area. She'd purposefully not told Conner that she was seeing Randolph's attorney again. She didn't want him to come and try to talk her into taking part of his and William's inheritances. She knew that somehow the Lord would see to her needs. She would not go back to the old life she'd left only ten months ago. She would starve to death first. Death didn't scare her like it once had. If she died, she knew she'd go to heaven and see Jesus. No one would miss her here on earth.

The door to Mr. Benton's office opened. A man exited with Mr. Benton. They shook hands, and the man left. Mr. Benton turned to her. "Sorry for keeping you waiting, Mrs. Carlyle. Please come in."

She entered and sat in the offered chair.

Mr. Benton rounded his desk and sat. "How are you doing today?"

"Fine, thank you."

"Have you considered my proposal to petition the court to uphold Randolph's unsigned will?"

"I have, and I still decline." She felt bad enough deceiving Randolph without trying to steal from Conner and William. They were both good men, very good men, and both deserved every penny Randolph had left them. She'd prayed and didn't believe the Lord wanted her to pursue action against the will.

"Very well."

That was it? He wasn't going to try to persuade her? "If you were going to so easily accept my refusal, why have me come down to your office?"

"I have other business to discuss with you. It is that other business that allows me to accept your decision so readily." Mr. Benton shuffled papers on his desk. "Which to cover first?"

First? What was going on?

"It has come to my attention that a bank account has been left in your name. This letter came from Northwest Bank." Mr. Benton handed her a letter.

She read the letter that indeed detailed she had an account in her name. "Why send this to you instead of me?"

"It's much easier to deal with me than a distraught widow."

She was far from distraught. Guilty, yes, but the banker didn't know that. "Who would set up an account for me?" She also wondered how much was in the account but didn't want to ask.

"The letter doesn't say. When we are finished here, I'll take you over to the bank and help you get everything settled. I made an appointment with the bank's manager."

Mr. Benton took the letter back, set it aside, and picked up another paper. "I sent word to Mr. William Carlyle on his inheritance. I received this telegram this morning."

Tell Mrs. Randolph Carlyle to stay in the house. Make arrangements for her to use any money needed for household expenses until my arrival. Sending letter with further details.

"Your husband's brother is putting you in charge of his estate for the time being." Mr. Benton took back the telegram. "We'll take this to the banker, as well. It seems you are being taken care of, so I'll not worry about you for now." He stood. "Shall we go to the bank?"

She nodded and stood. "We can both travel in my carriage. It's right outside."

Once at the bank, she and Mr. Benton were ushered into Mr. Olsen's office.

"I just have a couple of papers for you to sign." Mr. Olsen held out a piece of paper. "This one completes the transfer of the account into your name so you will have complete access to it. I just need your signature at the bottom."

Mr. Benton took the paper.

She scooted slightly forward in her seat as Mr. Benton read. "Who set up this account? Did Randolph?"

"I'm not at liberty to disclose that information, but who else would?" Mr. Olsen kept his nose crinkled to hold up his glasses, which caused him to wear a perpetual frown.

Mr. Benton handed her the paper. "It's okay to sign."

She signed and handed it back to Mr. Olsen.

"How much money is in the account?" Mr. Benton asked.

The question she was hesitant to ask because she didn't want to seem greedy. She just wanted to know how long it would sustain her after William and Sarah came and she moved out of their house.

Mr. Olsen handed her another sheet. "This is the amount of money currently in the account. Each month, an undetermined amount will be deposited from Carlyle Shipping."

That was a significant amount. She could live on that if she lived frugally. So Randolph had set in place a means to take care of her even if he hadn't gotten around to signing his will. She didn't mind using this money, because she wouldn't be taking money from Conner or William. "May I draw on this account today?"

"Certainly. How much would you like?"

She gave him the figure. She wanted to have money to pay Abigail when she brought her finished dress, and that sum would pay her well for her services.

"I'll get that and be right back."

"Before you go, we have another matter," Mr. Benton said. He handed Mr. Olsen the telegram. "I took the liberty to draw up a temporary agreement for both you and Mrs. Carlyle to sign as to how much money she may withdraw to take care of household expenses. If this agreement suits you, she'll also need money to pay the salaries of the two domestic servants who were in Captain Carlyle's employ at the time of his death as well as other household needs." He handed Mr. Olsen another paper. "As you can see, the amount is rather conservative, bare essentials for the house. Mrs. Carlyle has her own money now for her personal needs. When I hear more from Mr. William Carlyle or his attorney, I'll have a more complete document to sign if Mr. Carlyle isn't present to retain possession of his affairs."

"This seems reasonable." Mr. Olsen signed and she signed; then Mr. Olsen retrieved the money requested.

She had Scotty return Mr. Benton to his office. "Mr. Benton, thank you for everything."

"You're welcome. I'll let you know when I hear from Mr. Carlyle. In the meantime, be wise with that money."

"I will." She arrived home to find Abigail waiting for her.

&

"Hello, Harry." She bent down to the boy's level. "What kind of cookies does Miss Maggie have for you today?"

He pointed a chubby finger at a dark spot on the oatmeal cookie. "Dat's a waisin. I love waisins."

"You eat as many as you like." She straightened and sat on the sofa with Abigail. "You have a very sweet boy."

Abigail smiled. "That I do. I don't know what I'd do if I didn't have him." She stood and walked over to one of the side chairs. "I finished your dress."

She patted the cushion. "I just arrived and would like to rest a bit before I try it on. Do you have time for a short visit?"

Abigail nodded and sat. Vivian figured that Abigail kept busy to provide for her and Harry and that her schedule afforded her little time to rest. She felt a bond with Abigail, and they spoke easily for nearly an hour. Then she put on the dress and came back downstairs.

"I love it. I would love it more if it weren't black. When I'm not in mourning any longer, I'll have you make me another dress." If she could afford it. The money in the bank account was limited, but she would survive on it. The Lord had provided for her, and the least she could do was share with someone else in need. She took the money she had gotten to pay Abigail from her handbag and gave it to her.

"Mrs. Carlyle, this is too much. I can't accept it." Abigail held the money back out to her.

She put her hands around Abigail's, tucking the money into her palm. "Please take it." She glanced at Harry who had curled himself into the chair and fallen asleep. "The workmanship is worth every penny."

Abigail threw her arms around her. "Thank you. I didn't know what I was going to do. May the Lord bless you for your generosity and kindness."

"He already has."

nine

Friday, Conner pulled the shade up and flipped his CLOSED sign to OPEN. A young man about seventeen stopped his pacing on Conner's boardwalk and stared at him through the window. What was it with people on the store's doorstep? First Randolph drunk, then Scotty twice, and now this young man. He unlocked the door. "You're an eager fellow. Are you heading to the gold fields up north?"

"Nope. I just came from Alaska, and if I never return, it'll be too soon." The lad wasn't particularly handsome, with a pockmarked face and red blotches.

"You didn't find gold?"

"I wasn't looking for gold." He cinched a brown leather satchel up higher on his shoulder. "I was onboard a ship. I came back by land."

"Ship would've been faster."

"I won't step foot on another ship for as long as I live." His voice was hard and determined.

"What can I do for you? Are you looking for something in particular?"

"I'm looking for Conner Jackson. Is that you?"

He nodded and studied the lad a moment. "What's this about?"

"I was cabin boy on Captain Carlyle's ship."

No wonder the boy didn't want to sail again. He probably barely got off with his life. Randolph would have seen to the lad's safety and that of his crew before his own.

The lad took the satchel from his shoulder. "He told me to find you and to give this to you." His jaw worked back and forth.

"You were on the ship when it sank?"

"No, sir. The captain put this satchel over my head and shoved me into a dingy." Moisture filled the boy's eyes. "Said I had to live and find you. That it was an order. He told the others in the dingy to get as far from the ship as possible and paddle for land as fast as they could. I thought he and the other men would make it. It just all exploded."

A tear escaped and trickled down the lad's face. Conner averted his gaze and choked back some tears of his own.

"Mr. Jackson, the captain said you'd pay me back for the cost to get from Alaska to here."

He doubted Randolph was thinking about money for the lad when his ship was on fire, but the boy had been honorable in seeing that his captain's last wishes were carried out. If this really were from Randolph, he would pay the lad well. "Let me see what you brought." He pulled out the ship's log and a ledger book as well as a flat pouch with cash in it. There was no way to know how much had been in there, but the lad had to have brought at least most of it. The ledger was a copy of Randolph's shipping business's finances. He would take this over to his accountant right away and have him compare it to the ones from the shipping office.

Tears welled in his eyes. Randolph had known he wasn't going to make it, or why else would he have sent the lad off with this satchel? He took a deep breath and blinked several times before turning back. "Have you eaten breakfast?"

The lad shook his head.

"You like peaches?"

The lad nodded.

Conner took a can off the shelf and opened it with an opener from behind the counter. He handed it to the lad, along with a fork from a small stash he kept behind the counter. "I'll get you something more after my assistant arrives."

The lad was shoving the peach sections into his mouth as

fast as he could get them out of the can. He better get this boy something else, or he might start eating the can. Conner ran upstairs for a bowl, spoon, and a bottle of milk. When he came back, Martin was glaring at the boy, whose name he didn't know. "Martin, it's all right."

Martin nodded and walked to the back to hang up his coat.

"What's your name?"

"Todd Major."

"Do you like shredded wheat?"

"Heard of it, but I never had it."

He poured the boy a bowl full. "You'll like it."

The lad had downed one bowl and started on his next before the first customer crossed the threshold. Martin assisted the man in the pale blue coat. Conner went to Todd. "Do you have a place to stay?"

"No, sir." A drop of milk sat contentedly on Todd's chin.

This lad was trustworthy, or he wouldn't have bothered to come all this way on his dead captain's mission half starved with a pouch of cash. "You looking for a job?"

Todd shrugged. "It depends on how much it's worth to you what I brought you."

"Depends on what?"

"If it's enough to make it down to California. If not, I'll go as far as I can and pick up odd jobs along the way. People can always use a strong back."

"Is that how you came down from Alaska? Odd jobs?"

"Yes, sir. I hear California is a sunny place. No snow, either."

Conner handed Todd a piece of paper and pencil. "Write down how much money you spent to get from Alaska to here."

Todd pushed the paper away. "I don't know no reading or writing."

But he spoke well enough. "Can you tell me what you spent?"

Todd listed off every place he worked, how much they paid

him, and every place he spent money along with how much. The boy had a good memory. With a little tutoring, he could learn to read and write easily enough.

Conner filled a knapsack with food, gave the boy a new pair of Levis and a shirt, reimbursed him for his trip from Alaska, and paid him well enough that he shouldn't have any trouble reaching California. "If you decide to stay in town or come back this way, let me know."

Todd nodded, slung the pack onto his back, thanked him, and walked out the door.

Martin said, "Who was that?"

"Someone I wouldn't mind hiring. He was on Randolph's ship and brought me his logbook and a few other things. I'm going to go in the back and look through this. Let me know if we get busy and you need me out front. Owen and Hansel said they'd be in to work. We'll see if they show."

He first read the last entry in Randolph's log:

29 September
  I don't like the looks of the clouds boiling in the north-
western sky. The wind blew all night, rocking the ship.
Hardened sailors who never fell ill were heaving over the
side but stayed at their duty. We are in for a rough day and
night before we dock. If we dock. I hope we survive.

Tears welled. Randolph had known he likely wouldn't make it. A seasoned sailor could read the sky, the clouds, and the water. Randolph had been at sea for nearly sixteen years— since he was fifteen. He knew all too well what he was up against. Conner would give up the chance he now had to have a relationship with Vivian if he could have Randolph back. He missed his friend.

❧

That night after a pleasant evening with Vivian, Conner worked for two-and-a-half hours at the shipping office, sorting through invoices and scheduling shipments, trying to make sense of the paperwork with the ledger from Randolph. His head bobbed forward and he jerked awake, causing a muscle in his neck to twinge. He needed more sleep than he was getting lately, but what could he do? He had his own business to run, and he had to keep Carlyle Shipping afloat until William could come and oversee the business— whenever that would be. And then there was Vivian. He wanted to spend every waking moment with her. But if he did that, both businesses would go under.

He looked at his watch as a yawn overtook him, so he stood and stretched. He would get up early, come back, and finish the invoices before he opened his store. Rubbing his face, he shook off another yawn. The night air would revive him.

He locked up and left. Drinking deeply of the cool air, he felt more alert as he began the walk home, but he knew he'd fall asleep the moment his head sank into the pillow.

He heard a scuffle up ahead and stepped into the shadows of the nearest building.

Someone said, "No! Let me go!"

"You're coming with us," a gruffer deeper voice said. "Tie his feet."

Don't get involved. Just go home. He knew what was likely going on. Men were often shanghaied and taken on board ships as unwilling crew. Usually they were too drunk to realize what was happening and just woke up the next morning at sea. But this was different. This man sounded stone sober, and he definitely didn't want to go. *Lord?* As soon as Conner opened his thoughts to his Savior, he knew he'd help the poor soul if he could. But how?

"No! No! No!" the frightened, young, first voice said.

He recognized that voice, but from where?

"Shut him up!"

"Not on a ship!"

Todd! Todd Major. He definitely couldn't let them put that

poor boy back on a ship, not after what he'd been through. He peeked around the corner and saw them carry Todd bound hand and foot into the saloon. They would take him through the tunnel under the street and to the dock.

He couldn't confront them in the saloon or the tunnel unless he wanted to end up hundreds of miles from home at sea. He had to hurry if he was going to get a gun and reach the dock in time to rescue Todd. Martin lived a block away in an apartment. He ran there and knocked several times before he got Martin to come to the door.

"Do you have a gun?"

Martin nodded. "What's up?"

"Todd Major, the boy from this morning, was just shanghaied. I can't let them take him back out to sea."

Martin crossed the small room to a bedside table and retrieved a six-shooter. "I'm going with you." He pulled on a shirt and his boots.

"Martin, I can't ask you to come. It might get ugly."

"Because it might get ugly is exactly why I should come. And you didn't ask; I volunteered." Martin grabbed his coat. "Let's go."

Conner had to smile at Martin, only four years younger than himself, so full of virtue and gumption. He didn't want to endanger Martin, but he didn't have time to argue if he was going to save Todd from going to sea. A seaman's life was suited for a bold few like Randolph. Others chose it out of necessity or because it was thrust upon them.

"Three men took him into Barter Saloon. I figure our best chance will be to follow them when they come out the other end and free him before they put him on the ship."

Martin nodded and followed close behind. They moved through the shadows and arrived at the dock as Todd and another man were being carried over the shoulders of two men up the gangplank. They were too late. Conner wanted to curse but refrained. He ducked into the shadows and leaned against a shed wall.

Martin followed suit. "Is that him squirming?"

"Yes."

Martin sighed. "We're too late."

He could hear the regret in Martin's words. "They haven't sailed."

"We're not going to go on board?" A bit of panic crept into Martin's voice.

"I can't let them take him like this." It was one thing to go voluntarily as Conner had done as a boy, but to be forced. . . He had to think of a way to get on board without being noticed.

"Conner?"

"What?"

"I have to confess that I'm a mite scared."

Martin seemed to realize that if they failed, they, too, could be sailing for the unknown. *Lord, don't let us fail.* "I'll take the gun. You go home."

Martin shook his head. "Tell me what you want me to do."

He clasped Martin on the shoulder. "Thank you." He stared at him a moment. "I'm scared, too." He wasn't sure if he should admit that, but it seemed to encourage Martin. "I'll get aboard. You stay here."

"Shouldn't I come with you?"

"I think it will be easier for just one of us to board unnoticed. Two would look suspicious." He was pretty sure he could get on the ship. After that, he'd have to improvise as he went.

"How are you going to get aboard?"

Conner thumbed toward the supplies that would soon be loaded. "I'll hoist a sack of flour over my shoulder and walk up the plank like I belong there."

"What do you want me to do?"

"Keep a lookout." For what he wasn't sure, but it was comforting to know that someone would know what happened to him if everything went wrong. And he wouldn't be worrying about Martin's safety.

Martin held out the gun. "You might need this."

"You keep it. If things get messy, shoot it into the air. That should bring the sheriff and a few other folks."

Martin shoved the gun back into the waist of his pants. "Do you want me to go get the sheriff?"

"He won't likely do anything. If it was a matter of the captain's word against mine, it would be easier to side with the captain and let a boy no one knows sail."

"Then why shoot to get the sheriff to come?"

"Just a diversion. If we get separated, meet back at my store." He didn't wait for Martin to acknowledge his order but trudged out toward the supplies and hoisted a sack of what felt like potatoes onto his shoulder. Sailors moved around the dock and up and down from the ship, so he strode up the gangplank, half holding his breath. No one stopped him.

When he stepped on deck, someone said, "You, there. Captain's itchin' to get underway. Pile the supplies over there. We'll carry them to the galley after we set sail."

Conner acknowledged him with a grunt, crossed the deck, and set the sack down, all while scanning the ship to decide his next move and where Todd might be. Near the forward hold, four bodies lay. Three looked passed-out drunk; one, bound and gagged and squirming. He strolled over, pulling out his knife, trying not to draw attention to himself. When he was sure no one was looking, he knelt down. "Shhh."

Todd's eyes widened in recognition.

He slid his knife under the rope around the boy's wrists and sliced it, then did the same with the ankles while Todd yanked the gag from his mouth. Conner glanced at the other three men. There was no way to help them while they were unconscious.

Another sailor joined the one at the top of the gangplank and began surveying the deck. Conner grabbed Todd's arm and pulled him into the shadows under the stairs leading to the smaller deck above.

"Where's the boy?" the new sailor bellowed as he strode over to the three sleeping men.

Conner could see the feet of two more sailors join the first, who picked up a piece of cut rope.

"He had help. Find them."

Men scurried around the deck. Conner leaned close to Todd's ear and whispered, "I'm afraid there is only one way off this ship now."

"Dead?" Todd's voice was small and scared. "I'd rather die than sail."

Conner wasn't planning on dying tonight, but that was one option. He immediately thought of Vivian. If he died or was forced to sail, he wished he'd told her how he felt about her, but there was no time for regrets now. "Do you swim?"

"A little."

"When I start moving, we'll only have a few seconds to run for the side and jump."

"Will they shoot at us?"

He hoped not. "We won't be worth the effort." *Lord, give us an opening to get off this ship.*

Todd shimmied into his canvas pack. When had he grabbed that? He didn't want to fight the boy over it now, but once they were in the water, it would only weigh him down.

Two rapid gunshots on shore caused him to instinctually duck. Martin. The sailors momentarily turned their attention, and Conner grabbed Todd by the coat and dragged him to the railing; then he grabbed the boy by the pack and helped him up and over the railing. *Splash!* Shouts came from the sailors as they headed toward him. He dove over the side into the frigid black water. His skin tingled from the cold and nearly rendered him immobile.

He broke the surface to shouts from the sailors above. He heard four more shots coming from the shore. It was time for him and Todd to get as far from there as possible before the sailors decided to start shooting back.

Todd struggled to keep his head above water, flailing like. . . like a drowning man.

"Give me your pack."

"No. It's everything I own."

It was filled with the food and supplies Conner had given him that morning. "It's pulling you down. I'll take it. I'm a better swimmer."

"You won't let it go?"

"I'll get it to shore. I promise." He wrestled the pack off the boy's back.

Todd was able to maneuver better.

"Head for shore." Conner swam with one arm and pulled the pack behind him.

When Todd said he swam a little, he meant a very little. Even with the pack, Conner beat the boy to shore. In waist deep water he tossed the pack onto the beach and reached back to help Todd wade to dry land. Todd collapsed on the ground. Conner knelt beside him. "You okay?"

Todd nodded. "Mr. Jackson, I have a confession to make. I can't swim."

This lad had more determination than stampeding cattle. Conner had to admire that. "Well, you did pretty well. Let's get going in case they decide to come find us." He hoisted the boy up, and the two staggered down the beach all the way to the back of the store.

Conner dropped the dripping pack inside the door and opened the potbelly stove. Embers still glowed. He added wood and blew on it until flames jumped to life.

Todd bent down and petted Fred, who was sniffing him. "It's real fortunate about those gunshots. They helped us get away."

"They weren't fortunate; they were Martin. He should be at the front." He started walking. "Come along, and we'll find you some dry clothes to wear."

He opened the front door, but Martin wasn't waiting for him. Martin should have beaten them here. Unless Martin didn't realize he'd gotten off the ship already.

He turned to Todd. "Look through the Levis and shirts and find yourself something that fits. You stay here."

"Where are you going?"

"Those gunshots were from my assistant. I'm going to find him." He wasn't going to save Todd just to lose Martin.

He got to the building he'd hid behind with Martin and watched the scurry of men on the dock and ship. Had they caught Martin? He raked a hand through his hair. He loathed the thought of going back aboard. Escaping once had been a miracle. Escaping twice? Impossible.

"Conner," a voice whispered from the deepest shadow.

"Martin?" When he saw Martin stand and could make out a few dim features, relief filled him. "I was afraid they got you."

"They almost did. I scared a cat out of the corner, and they thought that was all that was back here. Did you find him?"

"He's back at the store. Let's go."

"You're all wet."

"We had to jump ship."

Once he got Todd settled in his own bed, sent Martin home, and got into some dry clothes, Conner walked uptown and stood outside Vivian's house. He could see her kneeling on the widow's walk, so he stayed in the shadows. What was she doing?

She stood and went back inside.

"I love you," he whispered into the night. Even though he knew she couldn't hear him, he felt better for having voiced it. Now he could go back and sleep.

ten

A week after receiving Randolph's satchel, Conner had read through the log. It spoke of nothing personal, only business about the ship and crew, but as he closed it, he noticed the corner of a paper sticking out from the back cover. He pulled it out. An envelope with Vivian's name on it. His heart skipped a beat. Randolph's last words to Vivian. His wife.

He couldn't forget that. She'd been Randolph's wife and still was while she wore mourning clothes for him.

He turned the letter over and over in his hands. What had Randolph said to her? Should he give it to her? It was in the back of the ship's logbook. Did Randolph mean for it to be there? The boy hadn't given him any message to pass on to Vivian. He did know two things: He desperately wanted to know what was in this letter, and he didn't want to give it to Vivian.

After he closed up shop the next day, Conner felt awful from lack of sleep. He'd waffled in his decision about giving Vivian the letter. When he finally had fallen off to sleep, Fred had spent half the night chasing a rat, which she caught and killed.

He saddled Dakota and rode up to Vivian's. The letter was none of his business. Whether Randolph knew it was there or not and whether he intended for Vivian to have it or not, it belonged to her. He believed that God had made sure it reached him so he could give it to Vivian.

Scotty was in front of the house, pulling weeds, when Conner rode up. "I figured it was about time for you to be arriving."

Was he becoming that predictable? "How's she doing today?"

He swung down off his horse.

"Maggie's not fussing, so Mrs. Carlyle must be fine." Scotty took Dakota's reins. "Go on in. Maggie's expecting you."

Very predictable, but as long as no one minded, he wasn't going to change.

Maggie met him in the foyer and took his overcoat. "Mrs. Carlyle's in the parlor. Go right in. Supper will be ready shortly."

"Maggie? Should I not come over every evening?" He held his breath for fear of the answer. Why had he even asked?

"You always came before the captain was married and then after he married, so why not now? He would like that you are looking after Miss Vivian. You were a brother to him. She has no other visitors because of the mourning time. It does her good to have daily company. It does us all good." Maggie hung his coat on the entry rack. "I feel better knowing you are aware of her daily moods. She's been doing real well since those first few days."

"Maggie, I believe her mental state is fine." Except for maybe not minding that she wasn't included in her husband's will—that still bothered him—but he'd taken care of it.

"Sometimes a widow looks fine, but something's brewing inside, and one day they just snap. I don't want nothing to happen to Mrs. Carlyle. She's a good woman."

That she was. "I'll tell her that supper is almost ready."

"Thank you." Maggie nodded and headed back toward the kitchen.

When he entered, Vivian sat on the settee, working blue spun truck into a mitten with four thin knitting needles. "Maggie says supper will be soon."

Vivian looked up through sorrow-filled eyes. "Thank you. It's so good of you to come. Please sit down."

How had he not noticed her downhearted countenance? Was it the will or something else? "Are you feeling all right?"

She tried to smile, but it didn't reach her eyes. "I'm fine."

Something was troubling her. "Have you spoken to Mr. Benton about petitioning the courts to initiate the unsigned will?"

"Yes." She set her knitting aside and stood. "I told him to destroy it."

He turned her around by the shoulders and heard Randolph's voice in his head. *Don't touch her. Don't ever touch her.* He took his hands away. "Why?"

"I can't explain it. I just know that things are the way they are as God has ordered them."

"Is that why you're sad?"

"I'm not sad."

"It's in your eyes."

"I'm tired of being cooped up, and when I do go out, being expected to behave the grieving widow. I am very sorry Randolph died, but I hardly knew him. I know more about you than I did my own husband. I hope you don't tire of my somber mood. I need your friendship even if it's only because of your loyalty to my husband."

"I'm your friend, too."

"I hope you don't think me a terrible person because I didn't love Randolph."

He couldn't tell her he felt a measure of relief knowing her heart wasn't broken. "I could never think you terrible. Speaking of Randolph, you know the young man I told you about from his ship?"

"The one you rescued, hired, and is now living above your store?" She gave him a genuine smile.

That's right, he'd told her. . .more than once. He needed more sleep so he could think more clearly. "I found this in the back of the ship's log." He pulled the envelope from his jacket pocket and handed it to her.

She seemed to pale slightly. "Thank you." She took it over to the writing desk and set it there.

"Aren't you going to read it?"

"I'll read it later." She put on a smile.

Of course, in private. She wouldn't want to read it in front of him even if he wanted her to read it aloud so he knew what it said and could see her reaction.

Maggie came in announcing supper was ready and breaking the tension that had shot between them.

He seated Vivian at the far end of the table, and took the seat across from her, leaving Randolph's seat on the end empty. . .between them, a reminder of who they each were and who they were to each other. He said grace, and they ate in silence for a while.

"Conner, I have made acquaintance with a widow in need. If I send her to your store, will you reduce the price on the food and other items she needs?" Then she added quickly, "I'll pay the difference."

When had she had an opportunity to meet someone? "No need. Give me her name, and I'll sell her whatever she needs at my cost." There it was again. In her time of loss, Vivian was thinking of others.

"So where did you meet this widow?" He took a bite of his roast meat, hoping the action would make his question seem more casual.

"Maggie found her, and I commissioned this dress. She's a wonderful seamstress. Her name is Abigail Parker."

So Maggie had met this woman. It would still be only a matter of time before Vivian met others or renewed old acquaintances. Some possible suitors. In a town comprised of so many unmarried men, she would have her pick of several eligible bachelors. He needed to make sure he was always close at hand to size up his competition. He needed to make sure Vivian continued to look at him for support.

❧

The next day, Sunday, Conner escorted Vivian to church. She hadn't been in nearly a month since hearing about Randolph's death. It was time to return, though she both longed for the fellowship and dreaded the false well-wishers. It was customary for society folks to leave their cards at the house of a family in mourning to let them know they were thinking of them. When she was up to receiving visitors, she only had to send word and the visitors would flood in. . .out of proper etiquette and not real concern. She wasn't up for their false niceties. She could put them off for at least six months. They would probably prefer it.

Conner had dinner with her and spent the afternoon. She was grateful for his company. He alone knew she hadn't been in love with Randolph and seemed to accept it well. She didn't have to pretend grieving more deeply than she felt. And she didn't have to feign politeness.

Conner stayed for supper, as well, and retired in the parlor afterward with her. He seemed hesitant to leave. She wasn't eager for him to leave, either. She was sure he had better things to do than look after her all day. His only day of rest. He worked too hard and looked tired.

"I've been meaning to ask you something. Actually, it's more of a curiosity. Randolph's letter to you—I'm not asking to read it, but I was wondering if it was a comfort to you."

"Oh that." She would like to say she'd forgotten about it, but the truth was she was avoiding it. "Um, I haven't read it yet."

He pointed toward the writing desk. "You set it aside. I'm not surprised you forgot about it."

Did he really believe a wife, even one not in love with her husband, could forget about such a letter? It haunted her. A voice from the grave calling to her. Condemning her.

"Would you like me to leave now so you can read it?"

"That's not necessary." She didn't want him to leave. This big house was lonely. She wasn't ready to step back into society. The only people she really felt comfortable with were Maggie, Scotty, her new friend Abigail, and, of course, Conner.

Conner left at the stroke of nine as was his habit. She stared at the letter on the writing desk, wanting to pass it by and continue ignoring it. She wasn't anxious to find out what Randolph's last words were to her, but she knew that Conner would ask her again. She couldn't feign forgetfulness again. She took the letter, went up to her room, and turned it over in her hands. *What do you have to say to me, Randolph?*

A knock on her door startled her. She shoved the letter under her pillow. "Come in."

Maggie entered. "I came to help you out of your dress."

She smiled. "I don't know what I'd do without you. Thank you for everything you do around the house and for me."

"It's my job," Maggie said matter-of-factly as she unhooked the back of Vivian's bodice.

"It's more than that. When William and Sarah get here, I'll highly recommend that they keep you on."

"You won't be staying in the house?"

She inhaled deeply so Maggie could unhook her corset. When she was freed, she could speak. "Captain Carlyle left the house to his brother."

"What about you? Where will you to live?" Maggie sucked in a deep breath. "I'm sorry. That's not my place."

"Randolph left me some money." She stepped out of the skirt and handed it to Maggie. "I'll be fine."

Maggie hung the dress in the closet. "This is a beautiful dress Widow Parker made."

"She does very fine work."

"Would you like me to turn down the bed?"

"No," she said too sharply, then schooled herself. "You've done enough. Go off to bed yourself." She didn't want Maggie to find the letter from Randolph.

Maggie nodded and opened the door. "I'll see you in the morning."

"Good night, Maggie."

Maggie closed the door behind her.

Vivian slipped off her undergarments and into her night-gown and dressing robe. She took the letter from beneath her pillow and sat on the red velvet fainting couch. Her hands shook, and she was suddenly cold. Determined to get this over with, she broke Randolph's blue wax seal.

Vivian,

I am a man torn in two. I long to be with you and hold you, but when I think of what you have done, what you were, I can't stand the thought of you. I have tried to tell myself you are not that other person, but I can only see you in the arms of other men. My mother was a harlot as you were. I could see no excuse then for her to do that, and I can see no excuse now why you should have done it.

I cannot reconcile this. You are not the woman I thought I was marrying. I can't live with you, but I fear that neither can I live without you. I have tried to come to terms with it, but I'm struggling. You have given me a weight that is too much for me to bear. What you told me broke me.

I will divorce you quietly and give you passage to any-where. I will also provide you with a small stipend as long as you don't return to your former life.

R

Vivian set the letter down and let the tears well in her eyes. Had Randolph stayed on his ship knowing it would likely sink because her secret had been too much for him to bear? She shook her head. He was a good man and a good captain. He would never abandon his ship, just as he wouldn't completely abandon her even though he couldn't forgive her.

She felt the weight of her secret lift from her. Randolph had released her, and she could tell Conner that Randolph's letter had brought her comfort, a sad sort of comfort. She could finally put her past behind her and remember it no more. Or at least try.

eleven

On Monday, Conner took Randolph's ledger over to Carlyle Shipping. Jonathan Kirkide once again showed him to Mr. Abernathy's office.

Mr. Abernathy stood when he entered. "Back so soon?"

"I just received some things from Captain Carlyle's ship. I wanted to compare this to the ones here." He held up the ledger. "Will Miss Demarco mind me interrupting her?"

"She's out sick today. Go right on in." Mr. Abernathy opened the adjoining door for him. "I have to go out. I'll be back later this afternoon if you need anything."

Conner sat at Miss Demarco's desk and found the most recent ledger. He tried to match up entries. After a half hour, he wasn't so sure that Randolph's ship ledger was a record of the shipping business. He needed to get back to his store, so he took both ledgers. Mr. Abernathy wasn't back yet. He stopped at Jonathan Kirkide's desk on his way out. "Tell Mr. Abernathy I have one of the ledgers."

The young man nodded.

He stopped by the accounting office that took care of his store's books. "Paul, would you look at these two ledgers and tell me if you think they cover the same entries?"

"I can't today, but I'll look at them later this week."

"That will be fine."

&

Maggie was boiling laundry in a large kettle over the fire when Vivian stepped into the kitchen.

Maggie pushed damp tendrils of hair off her moist forehead with her forearm. "It was awful nice of you to pay Mrs. Parker so generously."

"She did excellent work. She deserved it."

Maggie raised her eyebrows but didn't voice an opinion.

"Sometimes a person just needs a little help before they can get back on their feet. I don't want Abigail to despair." She took her basket out of the cupboard.

"With a friend like you, how could she?" Maggie stepped away from the steaming water. "I made extra scones this morning. The ones with sausage and cheese in them. I have some oatmeal cookies. Here is a pint of milk and some butter for the scones."

"Maggie, you're spoiling those children."

"Humph. I don't see how you can spoil children who have no home. You could bring them back here to live."

She'd thought of that. "They are good children, but what if they accidentally do something to the house? It belongs to William. I couldn't in good conscience do anything that might result in damage to his property. I'll just have to think of something else." She added some cheese to her basket and headed over to Abigail's home before going down to the water.

Abigail welcomed her warmly. "I'll make us some tea. I have some dried spearmint and rose hip from my garden." She headed through the living room with only a rocking chair in it toward the kitchen. "I've had to sell some of the furniture."

Vivian followed Abigail into the kitchen. "I'll help." It looked as though Abigail had had to sell more than some furniture.

"I'm sorry I don't have any baked goods today, but I do have some applesauce I canned." She took a jar from her sparse cupboard. "I could quickly mix some of this up into apple cinnamon muffins."

"The applesauce will be fine." She hadn't realized Abigail had so very little.

Abigail prepared the tea then brought two cups over to the table and sat. "I haven't had a visitor since before Harrison died."

How sad.

"No one quite knows what to say to a widow, so they say nothing at all. They give you a sad look and a wan smile."

Yes, she'd experienced a little of that the few times she'd encountered people. She was grateful they stayed at bay. She didn't know what to say to them, either. She'd thought she'd been successfully avoiding people. It seemed to go both ways. She took a sip of her tea. "I spoke with my friend at Jackson's General Store in town. He will give you a reduced price on everything you buy."

"Can he do that?"

"He's the owner. Just ask for Conner Jackson and tell him you're my friend."

Tears glistened in Abigail's blue eyes. "Thank you. It's plain to see that we are at the end of our means. To have my few pennies buy more food for Harry means more to me than I can put into words."

Vivian knew all too well how far a small bit of help went to strengthening one's hope. She would have to think of a way to do more to help Abigail help herself. Maybe find her a permanent job. "How soon do you have to move from your house?"

Abigail looked away, then said, "About a month. I'm hopeful the Lord will provide a place for us."

Which she would guess meant it was probably less than a month. Abigail was trying to look at things in the best light so they didn't appear so bleak. Vivian knew how that was. She wanted to invite Abigail and Harry home with her, but she didn't feel that would be right considering it was William's house now. What would Abigail and her son do when William arrived and Vivian had to leave? Abigail coming to live with her wasn't the right solution, but she'd take them in before she'd let them be booted out on the streets like the orphans she was on her way to see. "I have something for you. I'll be right back." She went out to the carriage where Scotty waited, brushing Honey. "I'll be ready to leave in a minute."

Scotty nodded.

She took out the five cheese wedges and went back inside the house. "Here. I know it's not much, but it will help."

Abigail took the wrapped cheese. "Thank you."

"I need to be going, but I'll pray for you and Harry."

"Thank you. That means more to me than the food."

She took her leave and headed straight down to the rocky beach. Everyone came but George. He was getting steady work at the dock, unloading ship's cargo. He was a good boy, and she prayed he would be satisfied with the work and not get into trouble.

Peter stood directly in front of her as she handed out scones and cookies. While the others went a few feet away to sit and eat, Peter stood, staring at her. "I don't got a tooth for you. I tried and tried, but none of 'em would come loose."

She smiled at him. "That's okay. I have something for you."

The others looked up expectantly.

She pulled out a penny for each of them. "And, Peter, I want you to give George his penny."

"Why? He gots a job. They give him lots of pennies and nickels and dimes, too."

"Because one of those pennies is his. If you keep it, you'll be stealing."

He nodded sadly, staring down at the two coppery coins in his hand. "I'll give him the not so shiny one, on account he has so many."

She knew George didn't just keep the money he earned. She wondered if he spent it all on himself or if he shared with the others. Maybe with her bringing food for them all, George would be generous, too. Then it made her mad. George was just a boy; he shouldn't have to be trying to provide for the other four.

Betsy brought over her fabric pieces. "I sewed them together just like you showed me."

The stitches were uneven, loose in some places and tight in others. "Very good."

"I even sewed a button back on Tommy's shirt." Betsy pulled Tommy over to show off her handiwork.

Threads stuck out from under the button, and the fabric was puckered where some of the stitches were too wide and pulled too tight. "That was very ingenious of you to try that without being shown." Vivian pulled out more fabric pieces. "When you are sewing these together, I want you to concentrate on making all your stitches the same size. Then sew these pieces to the ones you sewed before."

Betsy seemed eager to try, and soon the children scattered.

twelve

Conner stood in the middle of his store with Martin. It was nearing closing on Wednesday and unusually quiet, but he knew he'd likely get a last-minute rush. "I want to move all these center displays a little closer together so we can squeeze in more supplies for the miners heading to Alaska. I have a large shipment coming in tomorrow, and I want to get as much of it inside the store as possible."

Martin's gaze shifted from him and was clearly focused on the door.

He turned to see what had captured Martin's attention. A pretty young blond lady stood near the door, the reason for Martin's dumb smile. "Would you go see to that customer?"

Martin looked at him. "What? I'm sorry. What did you say?"

Conner smiled. "We have a customer. Would you go see what she needs?"

Martin's smile broadened. "Yes, sir." He hastened to the front and the beautiful lady.

Conner took a measuring stick from behind the counter and began measuring the floor space between displays. He wrote the numbers on the sketch of the store's floor plan that he'd attached to his clipboard.

"She asked for you by name." Martin looked downtrodden.

That wasn't his fault. He strode toward the woman, who now had five miners hovering around her. What a pretty woman did for business. "I'm Conner Jackson. May I help you?" He guided her away from the men.

"I'm Abigail Parker. Mrs. Carlyle said you were a generous man and wouldn't charge me as high prices as some of the other stores."

Ah, so this was the widow Vivian had asked him to help. "I would be more than happy to accommodate you. I'm going to have my assistant help you while I see to these men."

He went back to Martin, who was sulking where he'd left him. "Widow Parker is to have everything she needs, and only charge her my cost for the items, but don't tell her that."

Martin nodded lethargically.

He snapped his fingers in front of Martin. "I want you to help her."

Martin stood up straighter.

"Any time she comes into the store, either you or I will assist her."

Martin's smile returned, and he swaggered back to Mrs. Parker.

≈

That evening when Conner arrived, Vivian opened the door, glad to see him.

He held a box in his arms. "Your order. Most of it is here. The rest will be coming soon."

"I'd nearly forgotten about that. Just set it here in the foyer." She didn't want to open it now. She'd bought a pocket watch as a Christmas present for Randolph among other things for him. Maybe she'd give them to William when he arrived. "Supper is almost ready. Shall we go directly into the dining room?"

He nodded, looking so tired.

He sat across the table from her. Even after Randolph's death, Conner had continued his habit of stopping by every evening to check up on her. She made Maggie hold supper until he arrived so she could invite him to stay. Being in mourning didn't afford her much company for which she was glad. She didn't want to start socializing any sooner than was necessary.

"How is your business doing? There seems to be a steady stream of miners flowing through town."

Conner's eyebrows tightened. "You could only know that if

you've been downtown again. I told you to stay up here where you're safer."

"I could have heard it from someone."

"You haven't been accepting visitors yet, so you could only know if you've gone downtown."

She squared her shoulders. "I could have heard from Scotty or Maggie."

He narrowed his eyes. "But you didn't. You've been downtown recently."

"Don't scold me." Let him believe it was just once, recently. He would really scold her if he knew it was most days.

"I hope you at least let Scotty drive you in the carriage."

She nodded. "Maggie insisted." She wanted to get the focus off her. "So, your business is doing well."

He looked at her over the rim of his water goblet while he took a long slow drink. She could tell he was making her wait. Probably considering whether to answer her question or scold her. She was a grown woman of twenty-five, and she could go downtown if she wanted. She didn't need his permission, but for some reason, she wanted his approval. Maybe by having Conner's approval, she somehow gained Randolph's.

Conner finally and carefully set his glass back down. "Business is very good. Your friend made quite a stir at my store today."

She raised her eyebrows. "My friend?"

"Your widow friend, Mrs. Parker."

She couldn't imagine Abigail causing any kind of fuss. "How on earth could she have caused you trouble? She is the sweetest thing."

"A beautiful young woman like that? All she had to do was walk through my door." A smile played at the corners of his mouth.

Her insides twisted. Was Conner attracted to Abigail? No, he wouldn't be. He couldn't be. Conner took a bite of his chicken, still smiling.

Something curled up inside her. It couldn't be. But it was. She was jealous that another woman had caught Conner's eye. She lost her appetite and dropped her gaze to her plate, moving her peas around with her fork. "So. . ." She didn't know what to say without sounding jealous. "You were able to help her?"

"Once I got her away from the gawking miners and had Martin assist her. I told Martin to discount all her purchases."

She looked up. "Martin?"

He nodded. "You should have seen the way he looked at her. That man is smitten with Widow Parker. I hope she doesn't come by very often. I'll not get a lick of work out of him when she's around."

She smiled. "Martin."

He frowned. "I hope you don't mind me handing her off to him?"

"No." She took a bite of peas. Her appetite returned as quickly as it had vanished.

"Good, because I haven't seen Martin this interested in a lady before."

"Oh no. He can't be sweet on her."

"Why?"

"He'll get his heart broken. Abigail doesn't want a suitor. She's still grieving her loss and never wants to marry again." She felt bad for Martin pining for a woman who wouldn't be interested.

"I'll let Martin know to give her some time. Maybe he can change her mind about marriage." His words almost seemed to have a twofold meaning, but she didn't know why.

"I'm not so sure."

"Don't you think widows should marry again?" The intensity with which he asked took her back a little. He was a bit eager for Martin.

"It's not that. She was pretty sure of herself. And I was married before Randolph and widowed, so I obviously approve of marrying again."

Conner stabbed a piece of chicken. "Will you marry again?" He quickly put the bite into his mouth.

She couldn't tell what his interest was in asking that question. Was it simply because she was the wife of his good friend, or was it personal? "If the right man stole my heart. I wouldn't rush into it as I did with Randolph just for the security of being married." Would Conner protest if she decided to marry again?

He nodded but kept his focus on his plate.

For the first time, she felt awkward with Conner. "Did Martin get on well with Harry?"

He looked up then. "Who's Harry?"

"Abigail's son. He wasn't with her?"

He shook is head. "He can't be very old."

"He's about four. Will Martin care if she has a child?"

He shrugged. "I don't know, but I'll tell him so he's prepared."

"If Martin really wants to win Abigail's heart, he has to accept her son. If a woman has to choose between her child and a new man, she will choose her child."

"It sounds like finding a husband when you already have children has its challenges. But you won't have that worry."

She didn't need that reminder and wanted to talk about something else. "I received a letter from William."

Conner finally looked up from his plate. "What does he have to say?"

"He told me to stay in the house until he and Sarah can visit in the spring."

"Why so long?"

A smile forced its way to her mouth. "They're going to wait until after the baby is born."

"I'm happy for them." He pushed his empty plate forward and crossed his forearms in front of him on the table. "I know you asked me not to, but I wrote to William and told him about your being left out of Randolph's will. I know he'll give you what's due to you, as I will."

"Randolph left his wealth to you and William, and that's where it'll stay. I won't accept it." She had guilt enough over deceiving Randolph. His money and possessions would only be a reminder of her deception.

"I promised Randolph before he left that I'd look out for you. Seeing that you get your share of what was his is what he'd want me to do."

She raised her voice slightly. "You have no idea what he would have wanted." She didn't need Conner to force more guilt upon her.

"I don't want to fight with you, but if it's the only way to make you see reason, then I will. I will see that you are taken care of whether you like it or not."

"I have a headache. Good evening." She stood and left the room.

❧

Vivian climbed the steps back up to the street level from the beach. Only Betsy and Peter had come today. Scotty stood next to the carriage ready to help her inside. She had another errand she wanted to accomplish while she was downtown. Not really an errand, but someone to see.

"I'm going into Mr. Jackson's mercantile." Since Conner already knew she came downtown, he couldn't be any more upset at her.

"I'll drive you."

"I'll walk." It was only a block down, but Scotty drove the carriage on the street next to her the whole way. She smiled at him before entering the store.

A short dark-haired man with deep-set black eyes approached her. "May I help you?" He openly gawked at her from head to toe.

"Owen, finish unloading that crate over there." Martin glared at the shorter man then turned back to her. "I'm sorry about that. Owen is only supposed to be stocking the shelves.

How may I help you, Mrs. Carlyle?"

"I'm looking for Mr. Jackson."

"He's in the back disposing of some spoiled produce." Martin glanced at the three men who just entered the store. "I need to see to these customers. If you go straight back, you should find him."

"Thank you. I'll manage." Martin was a good man.

She found Conner hoisting a small crate and headed for the open back door.

"Hello."

He turned to her and smiled. "Hello."

That same feeling about him that she'd had last night warmed her insides. Last night it had come in the form of jealousy; today it was more of a satisfying comfort. "What are you doing?"

"Bad fruit and vegetables. I can't sell them, so I'm disposing of them."

She picked up one of the apples. It had a large bruise on one side but the rest was still good. "Some of this isn't so bad." She knew five children who would love to have all this wasted food, but how could she get it away from Conner without telling him about her almost daily visits to the beach? "There are needy people who wouldn't mind a bruise or two."

He set the box outside the back door and closed it then went to the window. "Watch."

It was hard to lean over far enough to see out the window.

Conner grabbed her hand. "This isn't going to work. We have to hurry." He pulled her behind him up the stairs to his apartment and over to the window. He pointed. "There. They're coming already."

She smiled when she saw Samuel and Tommy running across the beach behind Conner's store. She lost sight of them when they were right up next to the building, but in a moment, they each had a side of the crate and were carrying it off. Were they waiting for Conner to leave the food? Is that why they hadn't shown up on the other beach for her today?

"I don't know who they are, but sometimes there is a smaller boy and sometimes a girl."

Peter and Betsy. She knew who they were but thought it best not to reveal that to Conner. "That's very sweet of you to help out those children."

"I wish I could do more."

"To someone who is homeless, offering a bite to eat can mean everything." When Conner raised an eyebrow in question, she quickly added. "Or so I'd think." She did not want to explain how she knew that food was very important to the homeless and hungry.

Conner continued to look at her with one eyebrow raised. "What are you doing downtown?"

"Don't scold me. I wanted to see you." She wanted to see if the feelings of affection she'd felt last night were still with her today. And they were. That made her happy.

"I'll come by around supper. You shouldn't be down here."

"I have Scotty with me. I wanted to see if the rest of my catalog order came in."

"Since last night? I'll personally deliver it to you." Conner went to the stairs to take her back down.

She glanced around Conner's small space: a table with two chairs, a narrow bed, a braided rug on the floor. It was homey and had a warmth that her large house didn't have.

He led her outside and helped her into the carriage. "Please stay uptown so I don't worry over your well-being."

"I'm bored up there. I want something useful to do. I promise if I come downtown, I won't come without Scotty, so you needn't worry." But she could tell by the look on his face that he would still worry, and she liked the idea of Conner caring about her well-being.

thirteen

On Friday morning soon after Martin arrived at Conner's store, Conner went over to his accountant's office at Paul's request. "Something isn't right with these two sets of books," Paul explained. "I'd like to go over to the shipping office and look at the rest of the records."

"I'll take you over any time you want."

"I have the rest of the day to devote to this, so I can go now."

Conner put both ledgers in the satchel Todd Major had used to deliver the one ledger. He and Paul went across the street to the livery to get their horses, then rode to Carlyle Shipping.

"Paul, this is Jonathan Kirkide. Jonathan, we need to see Mr. Abernathy."

Jonathan's gaze darted from him to Paul and back again. "Mr. Abernathy's not here."

"Where did he go?"

"I don't know. He was here Wednesday morning when I arrived but left shortly afterward. I haven't seen him since."

"He's been gone since Wednesday and no one told me?"

"I didn't know what to do." Jonathan looked down nervously. "He's only been out one full day. Is something wrong? Is he all right?"

Conner had a gut feeling something was decidedly wrong. "Is Miss Demarco here?"

"She was here on Tuesday, but that's the only day I saw her."

"Come on, Paul. I smell a skunk." He strode down the hallway to the warehouse.

"Am I still going to get paid?" Jonathan called after him.

He ignored the young man for now. He needed to find out if his suspicions were true. Taking the stairs up to the manager's office two at a time, Conner went straight to the safe. The door was closed tight. Paul came in with Jonathan right behind him.

"I'm sorry I didn't tell you about Mr. Abernathy. I didn't know nothing was wrong." Jonathan's voice quavered with worry.

"Do you know the combination to this safe?"

Jonathan shook his head vigorously as though he'd been accused of stealing from it.

"Go back to your desk." When Jonathan just stood there, he added, "Yes, you'll get paid." *Provided you had nothing to do with whatever went on here.*

"Paul, the ledgers and other records are in this room." He showed Paul to Miss Demarco's office. "Here are the two you've already looked at." He took them from the satchel and handed them to him.

Paul sat behind the desk and began sorting through the mess.

Conner went down to the warehouse floor and spoke to the first man he met. "Who's the foreman?"

The man pointed to a broad-shouldered, squat man who couldn't have been more than five foot six inches but had muscles enough for three men. "You the foreman?"

"Aye, Collin O'Keefe." He had a strong Irish accent.

"Conner Jackson, one of the new owners."

"I heard we had a new boss. I was sorry to hear about the captain. He was a good man."

"Thank you. You look like you're still working orders."

"No thanks to the dandy." He thumbed up toward the office. "I've been going up there to find the orders. If you ask me, I don't think he's coming back."

"Why do you say that?"

"I haven't seen him since the other morning. He was acting

real squirrelly since Monday, like someone put clinkers in his drawers and he didn't want no one to know about it."

Conner had brought the ship's ledger over on Monday morning. "Do you know the combination to the safe in Mr. Abernathy's office?"

O'Keefe shook his head. "As far as I know, *Mr.* Dandy and the captain were the only two who knew that."

Conner turned away frustrated.

"But I could get a couple of my men, and we could blow it open."

He smiled. He liked O'Keefe. "Let me check with the captain's widow. Maybe she has the combination." He went back up to the office. "Paul, I'm going over to Mrs. Carlyle's house to see if she has the combination to this safe." He heard a rush of footsteps on the stairs and went to meet the men in the other office, the crowd of men.

O'Keefe had his hand on the shoulder of a beanpole of a man who was nearly a foot taller. "Tim here says he can crack the safe without dynamite."

Tim straightened his shoulders. "I always had real good hearing."

Conner nodded for the man to go ahead.

Tim knelt down by the safe and put his ear to it, slowly turning the knob, then looked back at the crowd. "Shhh." The full room fell dead silent. He went back to work.

Paul entered from the other office. "Conner."

The whole room turned to Paul. "Shhh!"

Paul closed his mouth.

Tim frowned, then continued. He pulled his head away from the safe, turned the handle, but the safe didn't open. He tried several more times, and the crowd started murmuring restlessly.

O'Keefe waved his hand. "All right. Show's over. Back to work."

Conner shook Tim's hand before he left. "Thanks for trying."

O'Keefe was the last to leave. "Let me know if you want my men and me to blow it." He walked out.

Conner needed to get the combination and see inside the safe but turned to Paul. "What did you need?"

Paul opened the ledger. "Look here in the binding. See that number?"

He saw the number eight crammed in the centerfold of the pages. "What's it mean?"

"I noticed them when I was looking at this ledger earlier this week." Paul flipped a few pages and showed him a number eleven in the crack then several more pages a twenty-six. "Those are the only three, and they don't seem to have a purpose."

"Unless. . ."

Paul smiled. "Exactly."

Conner knelt down and tried a few different sequences of the numbers in the ledger's centerfold until the safe opened. As he suspected, no cash. He pulled out a pile of papers and receipts and put them on the desk. "Let me know what you make of these."

"I'll come by your store at the end of the day and report what I find."

He shook Paul's hand. "Thank you."

The day dragged with few customers. Conner wanted to go back to the shipping warehouse but was afraid the store might get busy and overwhelm Martin and Todd. Owen and Hansel had signed on with a ship and left a week ago. Paul showed up at closing as promised. Conner sent Martin home, locked up, and showed Paul to his office.

"I haven't been able to go through everything, but it looks like it's as we suspected. According to the receipts, there should have been over five hundred dollars in the safe. I think there is normally more, but a large sum of cash was paid out for an order. I'm going to compare some of the figures with the bank on Monday. I think we'll find that Mr. Abernathy and Miss Demarco were taking advantage of the owner being out to sea much of the time."

"Thanks, Paul. O'Keefe seemed like a decent fellow. I'll put him in charge for now, and I'll be spending more time over there."

Paul left for home, and a short while later, Conner headed to Vivian's.

fourteen

Conner looked up just as Vivian glided through the doorway of his store. Was she trying to drive him crazy? *Stay uptown.* What was so hard about that? He would just have to be sterner with her. He would forbid her from coming downtown. It was for her own safety. With his resolve bolstered, he strode toward her. "Vivian."

"Conner." She smiled up at him, and his resolve melted.

It was so very pleasant to see her in the middle of the day. His voice softened. "What are you doing here?"

"I need your help."

He folded his arms. He couldn't look like the pushover he was around her. "With what?"

"I'm looking for a house."

He smiled. "You have a house."

"Technically, until William and Sarah come. I'm looking for a different house. Well, actually I found one. I want you to take a look at it and tell me what you think."

He leaned a little closer, and his heartbeat quickened. "I can tell you what I think: Stay in the house you have."

"Oh." She looked a little flustered.

Good. Maybe she'd stay where she was safe.

She straightened and seemed to pull her thoughts together. "This house isn't for me. I've sent a telegram to William to see if I can use some of the money Randolph left him to open an orphanage. The Randolph Carlyle Home for Children. I haven't heard back from him yet, but I'm sure he'll say yes."

"You want to run an orphanage?" She couldn't be serious.

"Not me. I want to open it and have someone else run it."

She better not be thinking of him for the job. He was

already juggling two, and not very well at that. "Do you realize what kind of undertaking that will be?"

"That's why I'm asking you for help. I know you have your store and the shipping company, but I was hoping you'd have a little time for this."

Time was one thing he needed more of not less of. "When you find someone respectable to run it, I'll help you." That ought to hold her off for a little while. Hopefully months, until William arrived.

"Mrs. Parker. She has a son to care for and is about to be evicted from her house. I've seen her with her own child so I know she'll be caring to the children."

"Children? Are you thinking about those two boys who took the food from my back porch?" It had evidently been a bad idea to let her see the needy children.

She nodded. "Sam and Tommy, but also Betsy, Peter, and George."

He couldn't believe she knew their names. "After I told you about them, you went out and found them?"

She opened her mouth, closed it, opened it, then pursed her lips shut.

"Vivian, what have you done?"

"I met them about a month before I knew you were feeding them." She gave him an "I'm sorry but not really sorry" sort of smile.

"Met?" There was more to this than what she was telling him.

"I've been taking food to them down at the beach. They're hungry. Someone has to feed them."

"You've been going down to the beach? Alone? How often?"

"At first it was just once or twice a week."

"At first?" He rubbed his temples. "Please don't tell me you go every day."

"Okay." She bit her bottom lip.

It was every day. He groaned. She *was* trying to drive him crazy. And doing a good job of it. "Let's wait until spring. I'll have more time after William gets here to help with the shipping company. In the meantime, let me feed those children."

"They can't stay out all winter. They'll freeze and get sick."

He rubbed the back of his neck. "Fine. Get the house, and if William doesn't want to spend the money, I'll back you."

"I want you to come look at the house."

"Why, if it's the one you want?"

"I want you to look it over and tell me if it's worth the price they're asking."

He took a deep breath. She'd succeeded. He was crazy. "Tomorrow morning, first thing before I open."

"Thank you, Conner."

"Now will you go back uptown where you belong?"

She smiled and nodded.

So much for being stern.

❧

Conner pushed on the stair railing going up to the porch of the house Vivian wanted for her orphanage. It was loose. The wood of the bottom step bowed under his weight. The front door stuck. Several windows were broken out.

"I know it needs a little paint, but Abigail, the children, and I can do most of it."

It needed more than a little paint. It probably needed a new roof. He didn't have time for this. "Why this house?"

She took his arm and pulled him through the house and out to the back. "It has a barn to put a milking cow, a chicken coop, a vegetable garden, and plenty of room for the children to run and play."

He could hardly think for her hand on his arm. He worked hard to focus on the building before him. The barn had no door, several boards were missing on the front, and who knew what kind of shape the inside was in. The chicken coop was broken down, and the garden hosted a variety of thick, prickly weeds. "This place needs a lot of work." And he'd likely be the one doing it.

"As long as the roof doesn't leak, Abigail and the children can move in and work on the rest later."

"And if the roof does leak?" Which he assumed it did.

"We can get a better price and have it fixed."

She meant he could fix it. "Fine. Negotiate a price."

"Me?"

"You're the one who wants the house." Vivian was a smart woman. He knew she could do this. She just needed a little confidence.

"But he'll give you a better price. He'll respect you because you're a man."

Unfortunately, she was right. And right now, the way she was looking at him with hope, biting her bottom lip, he could refuse her nothing. If he didn't start talking soon, his temptation to kiss her would overtake him. But then her black dress reminded him she was recently widowed, so he cleared his throat. "I'll go with you, but you make the deal. I'll fold my arms. When I think the price is fair, I'll unfold them."

She nodded reluctantly.

He strode back through the house. "Let's go." The sooner he was no longer alone with her and away from temptation, the safer he'd be.

❧

Vivian stole a sideways glance at Conner as she stepped up onto the boardwalk across the street from the livery. He'd left her carriage and horse there for safekeeping while they were at the bank. Walking down the street with him was quite an education. She'd always thought Conner a handsome man, but every woman they passed assessed him. Some boldly turned their heads to get a better look. Others simply gave a dart of their gaze. It didn't seem to matter whether they were in the company of a man or not. Conner didn't seem to notice any of them. Why hadn't Conner ever married? He'd told Randolph not to bring him back a bride. Was there a special lady who was unreachable to him? Or had someone broken his heart, and had he then vowed never to love again? If she wasn't wearing black, maybe he could see her as more than just Randolph's widow. She hoped no one stole his heart before she could shed her mourning garb. She slipped her hand in the crook of his elbow to let the other ladies know that he might be taken.

She stopped short outside the bank door and took a deep breath. "What if William won't agree to the children's home?"

"Then I'll cover it."

She tilted her head back to get a better look at him. Just like that? He'd "cover it"? Did he have that kind of money?

He motioned for her to go through the open doorway as he held the door for her.

The clerk behind the cage window adjusted his glasses. "May I help you?"

She looked to Conner to answer. He raised his eyebrows, waiting for her to speak. She turned back to the clerk and took another deep breath. "I would like to see Mr. Olsen, the bank manager." She didn't know if she could do this. Mr. Olsen scared her. He always seemed to be frowning.

"Do you have an appointment?"

"No."

He left and came back a minute later. "Mr. Olsen has an opening tomorrow at one."

She looked up at Conner to see if that time was fine with him. His eyes were narrowed at the clerk, and he folded his arms. Did that mean she wasn't supposed to accept that? "I'd really like to see him today?" Her nerves made her words come out like a question. She wished she could take them back and try again.

The clerk seemed intimidated by Conner and left again. When he returned a moment later, he was on their side of the cage windows. "Right this way." He led them into the manager's office.

Frowning, Mr. Olsen stood, pressing the bridge of his glasses higher on his wrinkled nose. "Mrs. Carlyle, please do have a seat."

She sat.

"Mr. Jackson, won't you have a seat?"

"I'll stand. We haven't much time and need to get down to business."

Mr. Olsen kept his gaze on Conner. "What can I do for you?"

"It's Mrs. Carlyle who has come to do business."

Mr. Olsen raised his eyebrows but turned to her. "How may I help you?"

"How much is the house on Cherry Street?"

"You already own a house. Why would you want another?"

"I'm going to open a children's home."

Mr. Olsen narrowed his eyes in disapproval, then quoted a price that was twice what Conner had told her would be fair.

She wasn't sure what to do. "Isn't that a bit high?"

"It sits on five acres, but for you, Mrs. Carlyle, I can come down." He quoted a price that was still high.

Conner's arms remained locked across his chest.

She took yet another deep breath. "Windows that need to be replaced, the outbuildings are in disrepair. . .the whole house is in disrepair."

"I'm sorry. That's as low as I can go."

Conner put his hands on the desk and leaned forward. "Randolph Carlyle has done business at your bank for years, and this is the way you treat his widow, cheating her out of money for a rundown house that has been vacant for years?" He turned to her and held out his hand. "Let's go. This is a waste of your time."

She gave him a quizzical look but took his hand and stood. She wanted that house for the children. She would pay what Mr. Olsen was asking.

Conner opened the door for her.

"Wait."

She and Conner turned back to Mr. Olsen.

Mr. Olsen's frown had deepened. "How much are you willing to pay?"

She quoted in the middle of the range Conner had told her. He'd said to start at the bottom and work up, but she didn't want Mr. Olsen to laugh at her. Mr. Olsen countered. Conner finally unfolded his arms, and they settled on a price at the high end of the range Conner had given her.

"You drive a hard bargain, Mrs. Carlyle." Mr. Olsen almost smiled.

She couldn't have done it without Conner. They left. "Thank you, Conner. I have never done anything like that before."

"You did well. You were at a disadvantage. Mr. Olsen knows exactly what's in your bank account."

"But it's not my money. It's William's."

"He gave you power of attorney over it. And agrees with me that Randolph's unsigned will should be the legal one."

"Well, it's not."

Conner retrieved her carriage from the livery and drove her to his store. "You go straight home."

"I can't. I'm going over to Abigail's to tell her about the children's home."

Conner shook his head as he set the brake. "Did Mrs. Parker agree to run the children's home?"

"Not yet."

"How do you know she will accept the position?"

"Why wouldn't she? She's about to be thrown out of her house and has no family to go to."

Conner shook his head again. "I suppose there's no talking you into staying uptown, is there?"

She shook her head.

"Do you at least know how to handle a gun?"

She nodded.

"I'm going to give you one. Use it if you need to."

"I have one." She pulled her Derringer out of her skirt pocket.

He frowned at it. "That's only got one shot."

"The threat of one well-placed shot can deter any man."

He waggled his head back and forth. "Be careful."

"I always am."

Moments later, she pulled up in front of Abigail's house. A sign nailed over the FOR SALE sign read SOLD. She knocked on the door.

Abigail's eyes were red rimmed and swollen when she answered.

Vivian immediately pulled her into a hug. "How long do you have?"

"Three days. I don't know where I'll go."

"Get Harry. I have something I want to show you." She drove Abigail to the house she'd just purchased.

"What do you say to being the headmistress at the Randolph Carlyle Children's Home?"

Abigail stared at her, then gaped openmouthed at the house. "You're opening an orphanage?"

"If you'll run it."

"Where are the children?"

"I don't exactly know. But I visit them at the beach. They must stay somewhere around there, but they can't stay out all winter. Please say you'll do it. Those children need you."

"Can I see the place?"

"Of course. It needs a few repairs, but I got a good price on it."

They walked around the two-story house: a parlor, dining room, kitchen, and bedroom on the first floor, and four bedrooms upstairs. When Abigail stepped out onto the back porch, which needed a whole railing replaced, she clapped her hands together. "Look, Harry, a barn, and we can put in a nice big vegetable garden to feed everyone."

Vivian smiled at Abigail's enthusiasm. "You and Harry can move in immediately, and as soon as I talk to the children, I'll bring them here, as well. The children may have to start out sleeping on the floor, but at least they will have a roof over their heads. And I'm sure the children will help clean up the place. I'll see that the windows get boarded up for now and replaced soon."

Abigail suddenly hugged her. "Thank you. This is the answer to all of my prayers, a place to live and meaningful work where I can keep Harry with me." Tears trickled down her face.

"This answers my prayers, too, for those children. How soon can you move in?"

"We don't have much anymore. With some help to move the beds and bureaus and kitchen table, we could be packed and moved in a day."

"That will be perfect. The children will have a place to live for Thanksgiving. I'll take you home to pack and make arrangements for the furniture."

Vivian left Abigail and Harry at their house to begin packing and headed to the beach. She sat there for half an hour before Betsy came with Peter.

"Where are the others?"

Peter held his hands in his armpits to keep them warm. "George is working. Sam and Tommy went up the beach."

She handed Peter the blue mittens she'd knitted. "I made these myself."

"Gee, thanks." Peter put them on.

"Betsy, I'll make your pair next."

Betsy nodded as she held a thin blanket tight around herself. "I'll see to it the others get the food you brought for them."

These poor, freezing children. She'd gotten the home just in time.

Peter stared at her basket. "Are we gonna pray or what?"

The three of them recited the short prayer, and she handed out the food. "How would you like to live in a house?"

"Don't got one," Peter said with crumbs tumbling from his mouth. He tried to catch them and eat them off his mitten.

"Would you like to live in one?"

"Your house? I know'd what it looks like on account of George took me there. He said a rich lady like you wouldn't never want a poor boy like me."

Her heart ached for these unwanted children. "I'm going to open a children's home, and all of you are invited to live there."

"You mean an orphanage?" Betsy asked.

She nodded.

"Are you going to be there?" Peter asked.

"No, but I found a really nice lady to take care of all of you."

"I don't like no orphanage ladies." Peter shoved his hands, mittens and all, into his pockets.

"Why? Have you lived in an orphanage before?"

"Nope, but George told me all about mean people at orphanages. I don't want to be chained in the root cellar with the rats and fed only bread and water if they remember to feed me at all."

Apparently, quiet George was quite the storyteller. "Mrs. Parker isn't like that. She's very kind. I promise she won't chain you in the cellar. She may make you scrub behind your ears."

Peter scrunched up his face.

"She has a son just about your age."

He widened his big brown eyes in interest.

These children needed more, so much more than just a roof over their heads.

ઠ

Conner felt a tap on his shoulder. He turned from his customer to Martin.

"I'll help Mr. Fink. You're needed over there." Martin thumbed toward the front of the store.

Vivian stood with a young girl of about ten with a dirt-smudged face and dressed in ragged clothes. He recognized her as one of the children who had come to get food from his back porch on occasion and walked over to them. "Who is this lovely lady?"

The girl looked away, turning pink in the cheeks.

Vivian put an arm around her shoulders. "This is Betsy. She's going to live at the children's home."

Was she the only one? He'd thought Vivian said there were five children. Before he could ask how he could help them, Vivian spoke again.

"I need your help. The boys won't come. They would rather freeze to death this winter." Vivian's eyes were wide with concern.

"What do you think I can do?" He raked a hand through his hair. She was the one who knew the children; he'd only left food for them on his back porch.

"Talk to them. Maybe they'll listen to you."

If all the children didn't go to the home, Vivian would go back to the beach every day to feed them. It was in his best interest to see she didn't feel like she had to. He couldn't believe it when she had told him she'd been going down almost daily to the beach. . .by herself.

"I need to wait for Finn to get back from a delivery, then Martin and Todd can handle the store for a little while with Finn here to help." A warmth wrapped around his heart at her look of appreciation and relief.

"I'll take Betsy over to the home and come back."

He could read in her eyes that she didn't want Betsy to change her mind. He watched the door long after she'd left.

An hour or so later, Finn was back, business was slow, and Vivian walked back through his door. He called, "Let me grab my coat." He got it from the back and headed out the door with her.

When they arrived on the beach, Vivian sat on a drift log, and he stood next to her. "Do you think they will come?"

"I told Peter I would be back and that he should bring the other boys." Her eyes widened. "Oh look, here he comes." Disappointment crossed her fine features. "He's alone."

He turned and watched the boy approach slowly.

Peter stopped twenty feet away. "Who's he?"

"He's a friend of mine," Vivian said. "You can come closer."

Peter shook his head. "He might grab me and take me away."

Someone must have told this small tyke tales, so Conner sat on the log next to Vivian. "I promise not to grab you."

Peter stayed where he was. "What do you want?"

He could understand Peter's lack of trust all too well. The image of his mother's painted face popped into his thoughts. He pushed it away immediately. "I know you. Did you know that?"

Peter scrunched up his face and shook his head.

"I own the general store. You are one of the children who come and take food from my back steps."

Peter backed up a few steps. "We didn't steal nothing."

"I know. I left that food for you." He remembered what it was like to always have that empty, hungry pain in the pit of his stomach, wondering if it would ever go away. Pain so bad he had wondered if his gut was eating him from the inside out.

"You gived it to us on purpose?"

"I did."

Peter walked over and sat on the log next to Conner. "I liked the sweet bread best." Peter hadn't been an orphan so long that he was incapable of trusting adults.

"Where are Sam, Tommy, and George?" Vivian asked.

"Sam and Tommy are under the dock." He pointed to the shadows under the dock on the other end of the beach. "They won't come on account he's here. George said he ain't never going to an orphanage again so there ain't no point."

So George was the leader of this little band of wayward children and the one who'd told them tales. "Will you go tell Sam and Tommy I'd like to talk to them?"

"Won't do no good. They won't go to an orphanage, neither." Peter leaned closer to him. "I like you. You didn't grab me or nothing."

He stifled a chuckle and reached into his pocket, pulled out a nickel, and handed it to Peter. "You tell Sam and Tommy I'll give them each one if they come over and talk to me."

Peter looked up at him with one eye squinted shut. "You got more of these?"

He pulled out two more nickels.

Peter's eyes rounded. He scooted off the log and ran across the sand shouting. "Sam, Tommy, you gotta come! Look what I got!"

Two boys came out from the shadows and gawked at Peter's nickel. The threesome started walking in their direction, Peter in front and Tommy and Sam cautiously behind.

"You sure know how to get to those boys. I knew you'd be able to make them come."

Conner was bolstered by Vivian's confidence in him but wouldn't kid himself. "They're only coming over to get money." He wanted so very much to please Vivian and to help these poor children.

She nodded. "But once they are here, you'll win them over." She smiled at him, and his heart tripled its beat.

Sam and Tommy stopped at the same place Peter had stopped when he first arrived, but Peter came over and sat next to him. "They don't believe you got another nickel. I told them you had two."

Conner opened his hand to reveal two nickels on his palm, then closed it. "First, I want to tell you about the children's home. It's a two-story house and has room for all of you. Widow Parker will look after you and cook for you."

The younger of the two boys licked his lips. "Every day?"

"Every day. Three meals a day. Would you like that?"

The younger one nodded, and the older one shook his shoulder. "We ain't going there, Tommy."

"I want to eat every day," Tommy whined.

"We ain't going. He could be lying to us. George said not to trust no growed-up people."

Conner needed to talk to George. He obviously had filled their heads with terrible stories of orphanages, stories that he himself knew were probably true.

"Come on, Tommy." Sam turned to leave.

"But I didn't get my nickel."

"He ain't gonna give us nothing."

"I will, too." He flipped one nickel into the air toward Tommy. The boy missed it but plucked it out of the sand. Conner flipped the second one to Sam. Sam caught it and stared at him. "I have another nickel for each of you if you talk George into coming to my store and talking to me."

They exchanged glances and ran off.

Peter jumped off the log and faced him. "Me, too, mister? Me, too?"

He smiled. "Of course, you, too."

Peter ran off across the beach as fast as his little feet would plow through the loose sand. "Wait. I'm comin'."

After the three boys were out of sight, Conner turned to Vivian. A tear trickled down her cheek. He brushed it away. "Don't give up. George is the key. I'll talk to him. I'll convince him everything will be okay."

She sniffled. "I know it will be. George will listen to you. I just know it."

He mentally kicked himself. How was he ever going to convince this boy who was set against it? *Lord, You and I both know I'm doing this mostly to win Vivian's heart, but I do want to help these children, too. I just never would have thought to do anything more than set food out for them. Soften George's heart for the sake of the other children.*

fifteen

The next day, Conner's store was teeming with customers when he saw an unkempt boy of about fourteen enter, looking quite uncomfortable. He hoped this was George and didn't want the boy to get away, so he quickly finished ringing up his current customer and hurried over to the boy. "Are you George?"

George nodded.

"I'm Conner Jackson." He held out his hand to the boy.

George stared at his hand a moment before he shook it. "I'm not going to no orphanage. I only came so the others can get their nickels."

As he suspected, George looked out for the others. He could use that to sway him. "Winter is coming on. I think this might be a cold one. We might even get a little snow. It won't be good for those kids to be out in the cold."

"We'll manage."

"Have you been in an orphanage where you were treated poorly?"

George looked down shyly. "I don't want that to happen to the others what happened to me."

"That's very responsible of you. But Widow Parker is not going to treat anyone poorly. She is a very nice woman who is as much in need as all of you. She has a son and she loves children."

"You could just be saying that. Grown-ups say a lot of things they don't mean."

True, but he had to win George over to get the others. "If Widow Parker and the children's home isn't everything I've told you, you and the others can leave."

"You don't leave no orphanage once they got you. You have to escape like I did."

"There are no bars on the windows, no fence around the grounds. You and the others can leave any time you like."

George just stared at him.

Conner reached into his pocket and handed the boy three nickels. "For the boys." Then he gave George two bits. "That's for you." He shook George's hand. "Thanks for coming. I know you'll do the right thing."

George seemed to consider that, gave a small nod, and walked out.

Conner had a feeling that George would make the right decision and talk the others into giving the children's home a try.

#

Vivian looked out the front window of the new children's home again. Where was Conner? He said he'd be there for Thanksgiving dinner. Everyone else was gathered at the children's home: Abigail; her son, Harry; Betsy; Sam; Tommy; Peter; Martin, who couldn't pay Abigail enough attention; Maggie, who helped prepare the meal; and Scotty. Even George was there. The only one missing was Conner. As she turned from the window, Conner came in through the kitchen door.

"Mrs. Parker, I have a surprise for you. Come with me."

Abigail put on her coat, as did everyone else, following in a cluster behind Conner and Abigail out to the barn. In the middle stall stood a black-and-white milking cow. Abigail squealed like a schoolgirl. "Thank you, Mr. Jackson."

"The children need fresh milk."

Vivian saw Martin scowl at Conner's back.

If she didn't know that Conner wasn't interested in Abigail, she might be jealous, too. But what if he had developed feelings for her? She would have to talk to Abigail about Martin and see if she had any interest at all in him.

They all headed back inside as a pack, and soon Maggie, Abigail, and Vivian had Thanksgiving dinner on the table.

After everyone had eaten their fill, Vivian offered to do the evening milking. Conner accompanied her, saying she shouldn't have to carry the milk bucket. Now she found herself alone in the barn with Conner.

"I think I made a big mistake." Conner sat on the milking stool, squirting milk into the pail. He'd taken over the job she had volunteered for.

Was he trying to win more favors with Abigail? "What would that be?"

"I should have had Martin present the cow to Mrs. Parker."

"Why?"

"Did you see the look on her face?" He shivered.

Yes, she had. It had been the look of deep gratitude. "Are you afraid of Abigail or of all women?" She hoped he wasn't one of those men who chose to remain a bachelor all his life. After all, he was twenty-seven, had never married, and had turned down her offer to have Randolph bring him back a bride. Now she was glad he'd turned it down.

"Only women who look at me with that glimmer in their eye of cornering prey."

"Are you against marriage?"

"No," he said quickly.

That was a relief. "Will you ever marry?"

He stroked the side of the cow and stood, picking up the pail. "If the right woman falls in love with me."

"She need only to fall in love with you, and she'd be the right woman?"

He cocked his head a little to the right. "The right woman would be the woman I'm in love with." He walked away, milk sloshing to the rim of the pail.

She stood staring after him. She wanted to be the right woman. But how did she make sure she was? *For one thing, don't look at him like cornered prey.*

&

Nearly two weeks later, Vivian headed to the children's home one afternoon. The roof was being repaired, and she looked forward to seeing Conner for more than just the evening. When Scotty drove her carriage into the yard, she saw Martin Zahn climbing down a ladder from the roof.

She took Scotty's hand as she stepped down. "Mr. Zahn."

He came over to her. "Mrs. Carlyle."

"I see you and Mr. Jackson are fixing the roof. Thank you so much."

"Just me and the boys." He waved his hand toward Tommy, Samuel, and Peter.

"Conner's not here?"

He raised an eyebrow at her use of Conner's first name.

She would pretend not to notice. . .either her slipup or Mr. Zahn's observation of it.

"He's at the store. Sent me over to do this job. My uncle was a carpenter in Port Angeles. I worked for him when I was a boy. I didn't much care for the work and came here. But I'm rather enjoying it today."

That was because he was sweet on the recipient of his labor. She would have to encourage Abigail to consider Mr. Zahn as a suitor. Vivian took off her hat as she went inside, then sat at the kitchen table and had tea with Abigail. "I didn't see George outside helping Mr. Zahn." She was hoping to start a conversation about Mr. Zahn to gauge Abigail's interest in him.

"George left three days ago." Abigail took a sip of her tea.

"No." The boy needed a roof over his head.

Abigail's teacup clinked on the saucer as she set it down. "He signed on a ship. I got up when I heard someone stirring during the night. George was packed and preparing to walk out the door."

"Did you try to stop him?" She'd worked so hard to put a roof over all these children's heads.

Abigail shook her head. "His mind was made up. I cooked him some eggs. I didn't want him going off on an empty stomach."

Tears stung the back of her eyes. "Who will leave next?"

Abigail covered one of Vivian's hands with her own. "George told me this was a fine home, but he just didn't have a mind to stay. He told the others that this was a good place, and they were to stay here. They all seem content."

"I'm glad to hear that." Vivian took a drink of tea and heard banging on the roof. "Mr. Zahn sure is working hard."

Abigail stood. "Come look what he's done for us."

She followed Abigail upstairs to the large room the boys shared. Four wood-framed beds lined the walls.

"Every couple of days he brings another bed he's made. He started with one for Betsy. Now she's in love with him. He also brought yards and yards of mattress ticking. Betsy and I have been sewing mattresses and stuffing them with hay. He also brought two hens and ten chicks the day after Thanksgiving, all laying hens. Come summer, and we have a producing garden, we'll have food enough."

It sounded like Mr. Zahn was doing everything he could to win Abigail's heart, and Conner was staying away. Both thoughts eased Vivian's mind and heart.

They went back to the kitchen and found Mr. Zahn waiting there. "I've taken care of the roof. You shouldn't have any more leaks. I'll come by after work and fix the railing and step out front, then get started on the other work, but Conner needs me back at the store so he can go over to the shipping office."

Vivian picked up her hat and pinned it to her hair. "Mr. Jackson is going over to Carlyle Shipping?"

"He goes over there at least twice a day and then in the evenings."

"Evenings?" He couldn't go in the evenings; he spent evenings with her.

"I think he goes over late at night. Stays until midnight or so."

So he went after his visits with her. No wonder he was looking so tired. He was going to drive himself into an early grave. "I'm going to Mr. Jackson's store. Would you like a ride?"

"I have his delivery wagon. I'll let him know you're coming so he doesn't leave before you get there." Mr. Zahn tipped an imaginary hat to Abigail and left.

"I better hurry so I can catch Mr. Jackson." She hugged Abigail good-bye and went to Conner's store, which was teeming with customers.

She directed a couple of customers to what they were looking for, then went behind the counter, where she knew Conner would want her. She watched Mr. Zahn ring up a sale. The cash register didn't look too hard to operate. "Mr. Zahn, if you would give me a little instruction on how to use that, I could ring up sales while you and Mr. Jackson help the customers."

Mr. Zahn looked unsure but showed her, then went about the store.

❧

Conner did a double take at Martin helping a customer. Hadn't he asked him to mind the cash register? He looked to the counter. His heart stopped for a moment. Vivian stood at the register, smiling at a customer. He strode over behind the counter. "What are you doing?"

"I'm helping," she said to him as she handed change to the customer. "Thank you, and come again."

"I didn't ask you to help."

"You didn't need to. You were quite busy. I asked Mr. Zahn to show me how the cash register works so he could help you out on the floor." She turned, smiled at the next customer, and began ringing up the sale.

When she was through, he said, "I want you to go home. It's not—"

"Safe. I know, I know, but you need help. Mr. Zahn told me you've been working here at the store and at Carlyle Shipping."

He shot a glare at Martin's back. He didn't need Vivian coming down here because he was busy. "I'm doing fine. When William gets here, he will share the work."

"Which isn't until spring. At the rate you're going, you'll be dead by then. I've decided to come down and help in your store every day."

"No, you won't. I won't allow it."

"If you're at the shipping office, you won't know. Excuse me, I have a customer." She smiled at the blond-haired man who eyed her with interest.

Conner raked a hand through his hair. If she were going to be here, he'd never be able to leave or work at the shipping office. A customer across the store caught his gaze and held up a can of beans. "Don't move from behind this counter."

She smiled at him, and his heart melted all over again.

When the crowd thinned to but a couple of customers, he went back to her. "Go home, and don't come back."

"When do you open in the morning?"

"Vivian, stay home. I don't want to worry about you."

"You're working too hard. Until William gets here, I'll help."

He raked his hand through his hair again. "If I hire someone, will you stay at home?"

She turned and faced him with a look of determination. He wanted to kiss her. Her lips moved, and she'd said something. He wasn't sure of it, so he swallowed hard and took a step back. "What?"

"I said yes. If you hire someone so you aren't working yourself ragged, I won't come down here and work for you."

He hired Finn that afternoon to look out for things at the shipping office and sent Vivian home. And although he hated to admit it, he did feel lighter knowing he didn't have to be at the warehouse all the time as well as at his store.

sixteen

Conner stood in Vivian's parlor, looking out the window at the budding bushes and trees. Winter had come and gone the same as the fall: cold and rainy. Spring was a nice relief with warmer rains and budding flowers.

He'd managed to keep both his store and the shipping business running smoothly over the winter months, as well as seeing to it that Martin had time to get the children's home fixed up. Mrs. Parker seemed grateful to Martin for all his work. Vivian had done her best to stay uptown at Conner's insistence, but when she had ventured down, he was always glad to see her. She'd started taking visitors but hated the falsehood in herself and the other ladies; everyone pretending to be friends and being glad to see each other when the society ladies didn't think her socially worthy anymore than Vivian wanted to be their socially snobbish equal.

"You're so introspective, Conner."

Vivian stood very near to him, smiling. He tried to not think about how it would be to kiss her and tore his gaze away from her lips.

"I have a lot on my mind with William arriving in a couple of weeks. I want to make sure the shipping office is in order."

"I can't wait to see Sarah and the baby. She wrote in her letter that she'd had a girl but didn't tell me her name."

It would be good for Vivian to have a friend her social equal. He should comment but was struggling not to take her into his arms. He flexed his fingers, then made fists again. He should leave now but found himself powerless to move.

"You'll like William." She shook her head. "I forgot you've known him longer than I have."

"I haven't seen him since he was twelve." But he'd known everything William had been doing over the years through Randolph.

"Oh, I didn't realize. That's a long time. He's grown into a godly man. And like Randolph, he's handsome. William, Sarah, you, and I can all socialize together." She stopped short and looked embarrassed. "I didn't mean to be presumptuous."

"It's not presumptuous." He wanted to say more but found his mouth unwilling to form words. Vivian's presence seemed to draw him closer. He should walk away into the night before he crossed a line that there was no turning back from and did something he shouldn't. She was still in black after all, a symbol of being Randolph's widow.

Instead, he took a step closer. Vivian tilted her head back and smiled up at him. That was his undoing. He leaned into her and pressed his lips gently to hers. When she didn't back away, he cupped her face in his hands.

He pulled away when the doorbell chimed. What had he done? She was still in mourning. He couldn't read her expression, and before he could say anything, Martin stormed into the room.

"What is it?"

Martin breathed heavily. "It's Finn. He got himself in a lick of trouble and is in jail."

Conner raked a hand through his hair then turned to Vivian. "I have to go."

She smiled and nodded.

He left with Martin. They arrived at the jail to find Finn lying on the cot in the cell, snoring. "Finn, what have you done?"

"He drank half the tavern then started a fight with three others." The sheriff stood beside him. "The doctor has looked after him. When someone pays the good doctor, I'll let him out, but not before morning, so don't bother coming back tonight. He'll be sleeping it off all night, anyhow."

"I'll be back in the morning."

Outside Martin said, "I'm sorry for disturbing your evening."

"Don't be. I'm glad you came to get me."

"But I spoiled your evening with Mrs. Carlyle. Are you going to head back over to her place?"

"Not tonight." The timing had actually been good. He had needed the interruption. He needed time to decide what to do.

"I know you care for her deeply."

"How do you know that?"

"The way you talk about her. The way you look at her when she comes into the store. The way you look at closing time when you're anticipating seeing her. It's the way I feel about Abigail."

"I can't hide much from you." He smiled. "How is Mrs. Parker?"

"She's doing well." Martin smiled now. "Those chicks I got her at the end of November have started laying, and I have the garden all tilled up. I'm going to see if she needs more seeds."

"It sounds like she might have softened toward you."

"She's started to think of me as more than just a handyman. She's invited me to supper a couple of times for no reason at all."

"Oh, there's a reason. How do you get on with her son?"

"He's been real shy. He sits off and watches me. I try to get him to help me, but he won't. He'll help the boys. Then last week when I was in the barn, he came up to me and said, 'My papa died.' I said, 'I know.' Then he took my hand."

"Sounds like he might have accepted you."

"I hope so. And Mrs. Carlyle? When does she come out of mourning?"

"I don't know." Conner rubbed the back of his neck. "I hope I didn't ruin things tonight. I may have been a might too forward."

"I thought I interrupted something. Maybe you should go back."

"I need time to think and sort things out." He parted ways with Martin and pointed his feet toward home.

Vivian hadn't seemed mad at him for kissing her—at least she hadn't slapped him—but neither did she seem pleased. It was as though she were stunned by his action. Had he ruined everything? He would apologize tomorrow and tell her he didn't know what came over him. She would forgive him.

❧

The next evening, Vivian stood in her parlor, unfolded Conner's note, and read it again. She'd lost count of how many times.

> *Vivian,*
> *We need to talk. I'll come by at 7:30.*
>
> *Conner*

Conner had never before sent her a note to announce his arrival. He didn't need to. *We need to talk.* Four words never sounded so ominous. She knew he wanted to talk about kissing her last night. Did he regret it? She'd been in high spirits all day until his note had stolen her joy.

Lord, please let Conner have meant that kiss. If the kiss was a mistake, please protect my heart.

The mantel clock struck the half hour. She sucked in a hasty breath, and her stomach tightened. The doorbell chimed a moment later. Maggie would get it. She walked to the window and stared out at the darkening sky.

"Vivian."

She couldn't turn around, dreading what he might say. *Protect my heart.* Conner was the one person she wanted to see most right now and the only person she dreaded seeing.

"Vivian." He stood right behind her.

She turned and looked up at him. *Protect my heart.* "Conner." She walked around him. "Won't you sit down?"

He took her arm and turned her to face him, then studied her face. "I've upset you."

She forced a smile. "Don't be silly. You just arrived. How could you have upset me?"

"Last night. I don't want you to be uncomfortable with me. I wasn't thinking. You're still in mourning." The lines around Conner's slightly squinted eyes belied his anguish.

Maggie entered with a tea tray. Vivian turned, grateful for the distraction. "Thank you, Maggie."

Maggie set the tray down on the table in front of the couch. "Would you like me to pour?"

Vivian was about to say yes so she wouldn't have to endure the awkwardness of being alone with Conner when Conner spoke up.

"We'll manage. Thank you, Maggie."

Maggie nodded and left the room.

Vivian wanted to call the older woman back but instead sat on the edge of the settee. "I'll pour you a cup." She tipped over one of the teacups reaching for the teapot. The cup rattled excessively as she tried to right it.

"I don't want any tea." Conner took her hand and brought her to her feet.

She forced her gaze to his. "Please don't say it," she barely whispered.

The V between his eyebrows sharpened. "Say what?"

Maybe if she kept it to herself, they could pretend nothing happened. "Nothing. The tea's getting cold."

"Vivian, I don't want to say anything to hurt you. Tell me."

She might as well, or she'd fuss over it in her mind until she made herself sick. "Don't say that you're sorry for kissing me last night."

He gazed at her. "What do you want me to say?"

She turned away from him. "I'm not sure."

He turned her back. "Tell me what it is."

Should she tell him what was in her heart? Did he feel anything for her? Would he think her an awful person for falling in love with her deceased husband's best friend while she was still in widow's garb? She should wait. "Conner, really, it's nothing."

He stared at her for a long moment, then took her hand and held it. "Come, sit." He sat with her on the settee.

Her stomach tightened even more. She could barely breathe. He wasn't going to let this go. *Protect my heart.*

"When Randolph first introduced me to his new wife, I was happy for him and felt he'd found himself a good wife. As I heard him talk about you and I spent time around you. . ." He hesitated, looked down at his hands, then gazed directly at her, "I began developing feelings for you. I know it was wrong," he hurried to say. "That's why I had decided to leave town, but then Randolph asked me to look out for you while he was gone. I tried to turn him down but couldn't. Please don't hate me for falling in love with a married woman."

"Never, Conner. I could never hate you. You have proved yourself to be a loyal friend and honorable man. You never in word or deed did anything to betray your friendship with Randolph or to go against God's teachings." To love her all these months and do nothing about it. Her heart leapt for joy. She reached up and touched his cheek with her fingers. "I've fallen in love with you, too."

He gave her a lopsided grin and just stared at her.

"Well?"

"Well, what?"

"Say something. Do something." She was suddenly nervous he'd think poorly of her. Why wasn't he saying anything?

He opened his mouth to say something, then closed it. He leaned forward and kissed her like she'd never been kissed before. This was the kiss of a man who truly loved her. Her heart exploded with thanksgiving to God for a love like this. *Thank You.*

❧

Vivian stood in the carriage and let Scotty help her down. "Come back for me in an hour." When she entered Conner's store, he was ringing up a customer's order and handing back change.

Conner came over to her immediately. "What are you doing downtown?"

"Maggie needs a few things for the kitchen." She smiled up at him. "And I wanted to see you."

His frown melted to a smile. "I'm glad to see you, too." He guided her around behind the counter and lifted her with ease up onto the stool. He kept his voice low. "I got to thinking last night that maybe I'd dreamed I kissed you and you said you loved me."

"You didn't dream it."

"You shouldn't have come down here."

"Scotty drove me, and I'm with you now. I'm perfectly safe."

He shook his head. "Not that. I've held my feelings in for you so long, now that you know how I feel about you and you feel the same, I'm not going to be able to hide it from everyone."

"You shouldn't have to hide it. Besides there has been some talk about town. People wondering if you've become more than Randolph's friend to me. Most people really believe you are Randolph's brother and that you only come around because you are family."

"But isn't it too soon for you to be openly courted? You're still wearing black. How much longer?"

He was as eager as she for her to no longer look the widow. "It depends. Some say a year, others eighteen months, while still others wear mourning clothes for two years. Abigail Parker wore her mourning clothes for only three months. They made her son sad. I think most people think six months is respectable enough. It's been about six months. I'll come out of mourning."

"Don't. Not just yet. Wait until after William comes. Let him see you are honoring his brother's memory."

"William knows I didn't love Randolph."

"Even so, for me, wear your mourning clothes until after William's visit."

She could wear black that much longer now that she knew how Conner felt about her. She'd been afraid that the black was keeping him away. "Anything for you."

He knit his brow slightly. "Except staying uptown."

She smiled. "You can't expect to keep a woman in love away from the object of her affection."

He thinned his lips. "See, it's things like that that will let everyone in town know there is something between us."

She glanced about. "No one heard me."

"Yes, but they could see that smile across the room, and they'll wonder why I'm smiling all day."

"I can't help it if I want to see you more."

"We'll talk about our future tonight."

Future. She liked the sound of that. She wanted him to take her in his arms and kiss her, but instead she held out a slip of paper. "This is what Maggie needs."

He took it. "Good. I need to keep busy while you're here." He walked off and started gathering her order.

Vivian picked up the Sears and Roebuck catalog and started flipping through it. The hour quickly passed as she pretended to look at the catalog but really watched Conner work around his store and help customers. She was fortunate to have a good and generous man love her. *Thank You, Lord.*

Scotty entered the store and came over to her. "You ready to leave?"

She wanted to say no but knew she should leave. "Con— Mr. Jackson has Maggie's order here behind the counter."

Conner came over to help carry it out to the carriage. "Do you have room for Mrs. Parker's order?"

"I didn't bring the wagon." Scotty hefted a sack of flour onto his shoulder.

If Conner had something for Abigail, then they would certainly take it. Vivian turned to Scotty. "Can't we fit it on the luggage rack in the back? We're heading over to see her anyway."

"Then where will I put Miss Maggie's things?"

She sighed. "We can't fit it all?"

"Finn should be back from a delivery with my wagon soon. I'll send him over with the food for the orphanage before I send him out for the next delivery," Conner said.

Scotty set the sack of flour back onto the floor and eyed Conner. "I'll tell you what. We load the food for those children and take it over now. Then while Mrs. Carlyle is visiting, I'll come back to get Maggie's order and take it to the house, then pick Mrs. Carlyle up." Scotty turned to her. "Will that give you enough time to catch up with Mrs. Parker?"

"Scotty, that's perfect."

Conner and Scotty made short work of loading and tying down the supplies on the luggage rack in the back.

A bawdy-looking woman stopped at the store window and peered in. Conner frowned and headed over to her. "I'm afraid you'll have to shop elsewhere."

The woman smiled coyly with her red-painted lips. "I'm only here to shop."

"I don't serve your kind."

"Too bad for you." The woman winked at him and left.

Vivian felt no twinge of jealousy because Conner wasn't at all interested in the woman. He almost seemed disgusted. At the same time she felt pity for the woman.

Conner was still frowning when he helped her up into the carriage. "I'll see you tonight."

"What was wrong? Didn't that woman have money?"

"I run a respectable business. I'll not have strumpets loitering outside my store."

"But she just wanted to shop. Isn't her money the same as everyone else's?"

Conner gritted his teeth. "No, it's not."

"But—"

"I don't want to talk about this any further." He walked into his store.

That wasn't like Conner. He was always kind and caring. How could he be so cold to that woman just because of her profession? She had feelings like everyone else. He had to have a reason for his strong reaction to that kind of woman. The kind of woman Vivian used to be. Would he hate her for her past? Or did he just hate women who were currently in the world's oldest profession? She needed to talk to him about it tonight, even though it saddened her to think his love for her might instantly die.

She tried to put Conner's reaction to the woman of ill repute out of her mind by the time she reached the Randolph Carlyle Home for Children. She was glad that Randolph would be remembered in this way.

Peter came running out before Scotty got the carriage stopped. "Miss Vivian!"

When Scotty set the brake, she held out her hand to the boy. "Hello, Peter."

Peter took her hand like a gentleman while she climbed out of the carriage.

"You have learned that very well."

"Mrs. Parker says being a gentleman is the most important thing next to going to church and knowing God." Peter scrunched up his face. "What's a gentleman?"

"Being a gentleman is being a good person. Treating people kindly and being fair." She paused to think. "A gentleman always helps a lady and never does anything to hurt a lady. A gentleman is always honorable. And a gentleman always lets a lady go first."

Peter frowned. "That's a lot to remember."

Abigail stood on the porch of the two-story house, holding a year-old girl on her hip. "Vivian, I'm so glad you came."

She touched the girl's hand. "Who is this?"

"Sadie. She was dropped off two days ago." Abigail rubbed

the baby's back. "Her mother died, and the woman who ran the boardinghouse they lived in won't care for the baby until the father returns. She doesn't think he will return."

Scotty walked up. "Mr. Jackson sent over a few things. I'll take the carriage around to the kitchen door and unload them."

"I'll get the boys to help," Abigail said to Scotty, then turned to Peter. "Get the other boys and help Mr. Scotty unload the supplies." When Peter ran off, Abigail turned to Vivian. "It's so sweet of Mr. Jackson to remember us and send food. Without it, I don't know what we'd do."

"He's glad to help. I know if he weren't so busy with his store and the shipping business, he'd do more." And busy coming over to see her. She felt her mouth turn up slightly.

"We've put in a garden, and when it starts producing, we won't need so much help." Abigail walked inside and motioned for her to have a seat on the sofa.

Betsy walked in from the kitchen. "Miss Vivian." She ran over and gave her a hug; then she pulled some fabric scraps from a basket at the end of the sofa. "Look at what Miss Abigail is teaching me."

It was a nine-patch quilt square. She turned it over. "Very nice. Your stitches are so much more even."

"I have seven squares so far." Betsy's face glowed with pride. "When I have twenty, Miss Abigail is going to show me how to sew them all together and make my own quilt."

"Betsy, would you go make some tea for our guest?" Abigail asked.

"Sure." Betsy put her sewing back and ran off to the kitchen.

"I'm teaching her how to run a household, so she can find a good husband someday."

This is what she'd wanted for Betsy all those months ago when she'd met the girl on the beach. "I'm glad she's a help to you."

"I don't think I could do it all by myself, and I do enjoy

having the company of another female in the house." Abigail caressed the baby's cheek. "And Sadie here makes three ladies in the house."

"Do you think her father will come back?"

"I don't know anything about him or where he went, when he's expected back, or if he's even a good man and father. We'll have to wait and see."

Sadie rubbed her face on Abigail's shoulder. "Someone's getting tired." Abigail shifted Sadie to her lap, holding her close and rubbing her back.

"How are all the children doing?"

Abigail smiled. "You'll be happy to know that George came back two weeks ago. I was about to go milk the cow when he waltzed into the kitchen with a full pail. He'd slept in the barn. He asked if I wouldn't mind him sleeping out there and having a few eggs if he did some chores around here."

"That's wonderful news. What did you tell him?"

"We fixed up a pallet in the little spare room. I told him since he behaved like a man, I wouldn't treat him like one of the orphans but like a live-in workhand. He liked that even though he knows I can't pay him. He's so opposed to orphanages. He's taken real well to the farm chores. He likes tending the animals and working in the dirt. He's dug irrigation ditches around and through the garden and built a trough to carry the water from the outside pump to the garden. Now if we don't get rain for a week, the garden can still get watered."

"I never really knew what he was like. He was always quiet and didn't say much."

"He still is."

Vivian was so happy for George. This might be the first time in his life that he had a stable place to live. "How are the others?"

"I've been inquiring after each of the children's families. I think I found an aunt of Peter's in Spokane. I'm going to write Miss Garfield a letter."

"How does Peter feel about leaving?"

"I haven't told him. Mr. Zahn promised the children one of Mr. Jackson's puppies. Peter won't be so happy to leave, and with a dog around here, I think it will be even harder."

"I'll ask Mr. Jackson if Peter can take one of the other puppies with him."

"What if the aunt doesn't want a dog?"

"If she's willing to take an orphan, don't you think she'd take the dog, too?"

Abigail nodded.

Vivian would be sad to see Peter go but glad at least one of the children might have a home with family. "How about Samuel and Tommy?"

"Samuel can be a bit of a troublemaker, and Tommy follows his brother's lead. George's presence helps keep them in line."

Betsy came in with the tea tray. She walked very slowly, staring hard at the tray, and set it successfully on the table in front of the sofa. "Shall I pour?"

"Thank you. That would be nice. You can leave mine on the tray for now."

Betsy seemed so much happier here where she didn't have to worry about where her next meal was coming from.

Betsy handed her a cup of tea. "Miss Vivian, I'm making mashed potatoes. Are you staying for supper?"

"No, I can't stay that long."

Betsy turned to Abigail. "Are we going to have an extra for supper?" Abigail nodded, and Betsy ran off.

"An extra?" Vivian took a sip of tea.

Abigail's cheeks pinked, and she turned away, moving Sadie from her lap to the end of the sofa. "Mr. Zahn is coming over for supper."

"Martin Zahn?"

Abigail nodded and picked up her teacup.

"I thought you weren't interested in having a man court you."

Abigail smiled. "He wore me down."

"You seem glad for that."

"He's a very nice man and God-fearing. I don't think Mr. Parker would want me to be alone for the rest of my life."

"What does Martin think about you running this children's home?"

"He doesn't mind. Enough about me. How have you been doing?"

Vivian's mouth stretched into an involuntary smile. "I'm doing well."

"What else?"

"I'm in love. I think for the first time in my life."

"Mr. Jackson?"

"How did you know?"

"Is there any other man in your life?"

She shook her head. "He loves me, too. He's coming over this evening to discuss our future." It felt good to share her news with a friend.

"Futures are good." Abigail squeezed her arm. "I'm so happy for you."

She was happy, too, but something nagged at the back of her mind. Something she didn't want to address.

seventeen

Conner stood staring into Vivian's fire. It helped him think. Today had started out perfect. The woman he loved, loved him back, and while he was thinking of her, she walked through his door. Then his past had reared its ugly head, threatening to devour his happiness.

"Is everything all right?"

Vivian's lilting voice drew him back from his haunting memories.

"I'm fine." He turned to her. "I'm sorry. I'm not very good company tonight."

"Come, sit with me."

"I'm too restless to sit." He rubbed the back of his neck. He had to tell her. "That strumpet stirred up memories."

"Did something bad happen?"

Something bad? His whole childhood. "Did Randolph ever tell you about his mother?"

"William did."

He should just say it. "My mother was worse, and I loathed her for it."

Vivian went pale.

He shouldn't have told her. It upset her. But he had to.

Vivian clasped her hands in her lap. "But she was your mother."

His anger at his mother leapt to life anew. "That didn't stop her from sleeping with any man who had a buck in his pocket."

"She had a child to support."

"That's no excuse. There *is* no excuse. From the time I was eight years old, I was sweeping floors and cleaning spittoons to feed myself. All she ever did for me was keep a roof over my head because she needed a place to bring men home to. When I was fourteen, Randolph got me a job on the ship he was working, and I never went back." He wouldn't go into all the horrid details of his departure.

"You haven't seen your mother since you were fourteen?"

"And better for it." He fisted his hands.

"Is she still alive?"

"I don't know, and I don't care."

"But she's your mother."

He shook his head. "She was just another tramp." He turned back to the fire.

"What about your father?"

"Never met him. I don't even know if she knew who he was. I was an accident and a liability to her."

Vivian came up beside him. "Conner, don't say that. She must have loved you."

"She didn't. She tried to kill me twice. I don't want to talk about her anymore or ever again."

"But—"

He didn't want to hear it, so he drew her close and kissed her. She fit well in his arms. He hoped Vivian didn't hate him for what his mother was. "Marry me, Vivian,"

"Conner." His name came out breathy.

"You want to marry me, don't you?" He held his breath. Did his lineage make a difference to her?

"Yes, I want to."

He kissed her again, relieved she hadn't turned him down because of his mother. He would spend the rest of his life proving to her that she made the right decision and that one's parentage didn't determine the man.

❧

Vivian didn't visit Conner's store again during the day and stewed for a week over Conner's reaction to the strumpet and what he'd told her about his mother. Her stomach felt like she'd eaten rotten fish, though she'd hardly eaten all week. She had to tell him the truth, but how? He would turn his back on her for sure. But if she didn't tell him and they married and he found out later, he would hate her forever. She'd tried to tell him after his confession, but the words stuck in her throat.

In her naïveté, she'd thought marrying Randolph would make her respectable. Only the truth would make her respectable now.

"Maggie, do you know where Scotty is?"

"I believe he's in the barn this time of day. I can go get him. What do you need?"

"I'm going to take the carriage into town. I'll find him. Thank you." She went out to the barn but didn't see Scotty anywhere. The horse poked his head out of the stall and whinnied a greeting by bobbing her head.

She looked from the horse to the carriage parked on the opposite side of the barn and back again. "We can do this, can't we?" She walked toward the horse.

The horse nodded and flapped her lips. She went into the tack room and took the nearest harness off the peg on the wall, then went back to the stall and opened the door. She held the bit in front of the horse's mouth; then she turned it over. Which way was up? "Do you know?"

"May I help you?"

She jumped, sucking in a breath and spinning around to face Scotty, stoop-shouldered. "I want to hitch the carriage and go into town." She held out the harness to him.

Scotty took it. "Honey don't like this bit." He disappeared into the tack room and came out with another harness that looked the same to her. When he got the horse all hooked up and hitched to the carriage, he said, "I'll change my clothes into something more suitable for town."

"No need, Scotty. I'll drive myself."

"Mr. Jackson isn't going to like that."

Mr. Jackson wasn't going to like much of today where she

was concerned. "I'll be fine. I'll tell him that you protested and I gave you no choice." She let Scotty help her up into the seat and drove off. A few minutes later, she pulled up in front of Conner's store.

Conner came out smiling before she could get the brake set. "What are you doing here? I thought I finally got you to stay uptown." He put his hands around her waist and lifted her down.

She put her hands on his shoulders as he gently set her on the boardwalk. "I need to talk to you. Are you busy? Can you get away?"

"I'll come by this evening and we can talk then."

She didn't want him coming by unless he wanted to after knowing the truth. "Since I'm here, we can talk now."

"I have a few customers to help; then I think Martin and Todd can handle things here for a little while." He guided her inside and started to show her to the stool he usually made her sit on.

She couldn't be stagnant. "I'm going to look around a bit." She picked up a can of this and a box of that without really seeing what she was doing.

"I know you."

She turned to a man with a long, curled handlebar mustache. She couldn't say anything. She indeed knew the man from her days in Coos Bay but didn't know his name. She took a slow deep breath. "You must have me mistaken with someone else." That was a lie, but she couldn't admit to her past like this. She'd thought her past wouldn't find her here. She was a new creation; her sins remembered no more.

"I remember that face." His gaze scanned the length of her. "And that body."

Why couldn't people be as forgetful as God chose to be? "No." Her voice came out small. This couldn't be happening.

The man shifted his gaze to just behind her. "Did you get yourself a respectable man?"

She looked back at Conner. The fury on his face said he wanted to rip the man's throat out. "Apologize to the lady."

The man laughed. "She's no lady."

"Conner, it's all right. Let's just go."

Conner stepped in front of her, his jaw set. "You have made a mistake."

"I've made no mistake. This is Vivian Miller. I've paid for her services before."

Conner squared his shoulders and stepped within inches of the man. "You will apologize to the lady, or I'll throw you out of my store."

The smaller man finally registered the potential danger he might be in from Conner. "Sorry, ma'am." The man hastily left.

"Conner, I can explain."

Conner pulled her by her arm outside and lifted her into her carriage. "Go home, and stay there."

"Conner, please."

He wouldn't look at her. "Don't come back downtown." He slapped Honey on her rump, and the horse stepped into motion.

Maybe Conner hadn't heard the man right. No, it was all too clear. Maybe he hadn't believed what the man was accusing her of. But the look on his face was so horrible. *Lord, give me the opportunity to explain to Conner. Please, please, please let him forgive me.*

By the time she reached her house, her vision was clouded and tears stained her cheeks. Good thing Honey knew her way home.

She waited all evening. Conner never came. She'd hoped he would but wasn't surprised. She went to her room and out onto her widow's walk. She'd never felt worse in her entire life.

&

Conner stalked the streets and ducked into every saloon until he located the man who'd come into his store earlier. The man sat at a table in a smoke-filled room, holding a fist full of cards. Conner walked over.

The man folded his cards and excused himself from the table. "I apologized to the *lady* as you asked."

"I want you to never repeat what you said and to leave town. Tonight."

"I'm heading up to Alaska. Won't let no one in the Yukon without a year's supply of food and such. I have to wait my turn."

"I'll have your supplies ready for you in the morning. You be gone by the afternoon."

"Vivian must be something important to you for you to be behaving this way."

He fisted his hands at his side. He wanted to hit the man real bad, but he wouldn't be goaded into a fight. This man was spewing nothing but filthy lies.

❧

Conner tried to ignore Scotty when he entered his store. Vivian had sent him every day for the past five days to see when he was coming by her house. He didn't know how to face her. He didn't want her explanation for what the man had said to her. He didn't want to believe what he'd implied. "Scotty, tell her I've got trouble at the shipping office. I just can't come by."

"That's not going to work this time. Mrs. Carlyle says if she doesn't see you tonight, she's coming down here tomorrow."

"Tell her that I really can't come tonight, but I'll definitely be there tomorrow night. I have a big shipment coming in to Carlyle Shipping that demands my attention. I will come tomorrow night." That should give him more time to. . .to what? Avoid the truth?

He sent Martin home, or rather over to Mrs. Parker at the orphanage; then he locked up and headed over to Carlyle Shipping. He skipped supper and was still entering numbers into the ledger when someone knocked on the office door. "Come in."

Finn poked his head in. "You have a visitor."

He stood and stretched. "At this hour? Send him in."

"It's a her."

His gut flinched. She wouldn't come down here? This was worse than his store.

Vivian crossed his threshold looking like an elegant china doll.

He wanted to go to her and hold her and kiss her. Yet she repulsed him. "I told Scotty I'd see you tomorrow night."

"We need to talk." Her voice quavered a little.

"Tomorrow. I have a lot of work to do." He needed one more day of believing she was Randolph's respectable widow. But he knew the truth. In his gut. Her face told it, too.

She sat in the chair opposite his desk. She wasn't leaving. He had to face this now.

He sank back down into his chair. "Vivian, please don't say it's true."

"I wish I could. I wish I could change many things about my past, but I can't. That's not the way I wanted to live my life." Her voice shook more.

He swallowed hard. "But you were a...a...?" He couldn't say it. "Like my mother?"

She nodded. "A prostitute. I'm not proud of it. I never wanted to live that way."

Disgust and anger rose in him, and he stood. "But you did."

"Let me explain."

"I don't want to hear it. Leave." He strode around his desk and grabbed the doorknob, but when she continued to speak, he froze with his hand in place, unable to look at her.

"I had no money and no place to live. I was hungry and sick. A man, a doctor took me in. He was nice to me and took care of me."

He wrenched open the door and turned on her. "And for that you sold yourself?"

"I didn't have any other choice."

He clenched his teeth. "There are always choices."

"I didn't know the Lord. I didn't know the depth of my sin."

Tears flooded her eyes, but he wasn't going to let them sway him. She was no different than his mother. If he could walk away from his mother, he could walk away from her. "I never want to see you again."

"I'm not leaving until I make you understand."

Then he'd leave. He grabbed the railings and took the stairs three at a time.

"I love you," she said behind him.

He tried to block it out but couldn't. He ran all the way to Admiralty Inlet, trying to outrun her words and his feelings for her. He reached the beach exhausted and fell to his knees. He cried out as his heart ripped in two.

eighteen

Vivian wrapped herself in a quilt and sat out on her widow's walk all night with her unopened letters to Conner in her hand. She'd hoped when Conner's anger cooled he would at least read one of them, but every letter came back to her unread like a slap in the face. This was the eighth night in a row that she had watched the dark waters by night and slept by day. Now she felt like a widow. Why couldn't Conner see she had changed? She wasn't a strumpet anymore. She was a new creation. Why couldn't he forgive her?

The eastern sky began to gray as dawn approached. William and Sarah had sent word that they would arrive today but not until the afternoon. She would sleep until then, so she went inside and curled up in her bed.

She woke to Maggie shaking her. "Time to get up."

"What time is it?"

"Three o'clock. Your company will be here in a couple of hours. We have to get you presentable."

She didn't care if she was presentable or not, but it would be good to see Sarah and William again. They would lighten her heart.

As Maggie helped her bathe and dress, she did feel better. She didn't even mind putting on the black mourning dress. It seemed to suit her now. Or at least her mood. She would have Maggie dye all her dresses black.

"Scotty has gone to the dock to pick them up as soon as they get off the ship, and I've fixed you a little something to eat and I don't want to hear no fuss about it."

"I'm not hungry."

"Hungry or not, you're going to eat. You haven't eaten hardly a thing in a week. It won't do you no good to be fainting as soon as your guests arrive."

She nodded and followed Maggie downstairs, but she was the one who would be the guest now. The house was William and Sarah's. She would need to move. But where? Seattle? She could find a job as a housekeeper there.

Vivian hurried outside when she saw Scotty driving up the carriage. "Sarah!"

"Vivian!"

William, looking dapper in his suit, jumped down and took the baby from Sarah, then gave his wife a hand to help her down. Sarah gave her a hug then turned and took the baby from her husband. "I'd like you to meet our daughter, Vivian."

She caressed the sleeping baby's cheek. "What's her name?"

Sarah giggled. "I just told you. Vivian."

"You named her after me?"

Sarah nodded. "William insisted. We have some other good news."

"You're having another baby?"

"No. We're staying in Port Townsend."

"That's wonderful. Come inside."

They sat in the parlor, and Maggie served them tea.

"It only makes sense for you two—I mean three—to move here. You have this beautiful house." She almost wanted to cry at the thought of leaving it.

Sarah put her hand on Vivian's arm. "We're staying to be close to you and to Conner. We know there are no blood ties, but you're the only family that either of us has. William can't say enough about Conner."

At the mention of his name, the breath froze in her lungs.

"Speaking of Conner, he wrote to me several times about Randolph not updating his will before he died." William took a sip of tea. "I agree with Conner that you should have a full third of Carlyle Shipping, and Sarah and I have discussed it and think you should have half the house, as well. We want to uphold the will that Randolph never signed."

Tears stung the back of her eyes. She had to tell William what she'd done. "I can't accept it. Randolph was right in not putting me in his will. I never should have married him when I harbored such a dark secret. I know you warned me not to, but I told him the truth just before he died. He was furious with me. He wouldn't want me to have anything." And Conner certainly wouldn't want her for a business partner.

"Nonsense. You're my brother's legal widow, and I'll see to it that you are taken care of. If my brother hadn't been so greedy to marry you, you wouldn't have had to keep your secret from him."

"I kept it from Conner, too, but he knows now."

William grimaced.

Sarah squeezed her arm. "How did he take it?"

"Worse than Randolph. He never wants to see me again." She turned to William. "William, you have never held my past against me. Why are you so forgiving and accepting when your brother and Conner aren't?"

" 'All have sinned, and come short of the glory of God.' 'While we were yet sinners, Christ died for us.' Randolph and Conner could never separate the person from the sin. They couldn't see that our mother and Conner's mother were wounded, sinning people like the rest of us. To them, our mothers were their sin. But God loves us all in spite of our sin. He doesn't rank our sins on severity. They are all putrid to Him, but He covered them with Christ's blood."

That's what she believed. "Conner told me about his mother being a prostitute, too. Why can't he understand that sometimes a woman has few choices?"

"His mother did have a choice. Our mother only did it for a while to feed and clothe us. Conner's mother chose it over honest work. She worked as a maid in the same house as our mother and quit to go back to prostitution because the honest work was too hard. She was mean and vile. I don't know if Conner has ever forgiven her."

"He hasn't. If he can't forgive his own mother, then he'll never be able to forgive me."

"I'll speak to him," William said.

"He won't listen."

"He'll listen to me. I'll make him listen. I've known him since childhood."

Could William really make the difference? She desperately hoped so.

≈

Conner sat in the Carlyle Shipping manager's office and held his head in his hands. It was getting late, and he had a headache again. He hadn't slept well since he had sent Vivian away—no—since he'd learned of her scarlet past. A knock mercifully interrupted his thoughts. "Come in."

A young Randolph filled the doorway of the shipping office.

He stood. "William?"

The man nodded and broke into a wide smile.

"You grew up." He came around his desk and hugged his oldest friend. Though he hadn't seen William since they were children, he'd learned all about what he was doing through Randolph, and since Randolph's death, he'd corresponded regularly with him. "You look good."

"You look like something the dog dragged in."

Conner raked his hand through his hair. "I'm having quite a time keeping up with my store and Carlyle Shipping."

"Where's Randolph's manager? Don't tell me you fired him?"

He shook his head. "I didn't have a chance. He and the bookkeeper ran off with the money in the safe months ago. Fortunately, there wasn't much there at the time. I'd taken most of it to the bank. I don't know for how long they were pinching from Randolph. I wrote you about that."

William nodded. "You didn't hire a new manager?"

Conner shook his head. "I didn't know who I could trust."

William took a deep breath. "Me. I'm staying in town. I'll run the shipping company for the three of us."

"Three?"

"You, me, and Vivian."

He'd forgotten about her being part owner. "I'd rather just sell you my share."

"I don't have the money to buy you out."

"Then I'll turn it over to you."

William narrowed his eyes and studied him. "Have you eaten?"

He shook his head.

"Let's go get something and talk."

Conner locked up the shipping office and took William back to his store, where he made some scrambled eggs and bacon. William didn't eat much. He'd probably already eaten.

"You have to forgive her, Conner."

"Forgive who?" He knew whom.

"Vivian. Your mother. The world. I can see that it's eating you up inside."

"Vivian was a prostitute." The word felt like poison in his mouth. "But you knew that, didn't you? Why didn't you tell me?"

"Because she's completely turned her back on that life. She's a good person."

"How can you say that?"

William picked up Conner's Bible from his bedside table and flipped through it. " 'For if ye forgive men their trespasses, your heavenly Father will also forgive you: But if ye forgive not men their trespasses, neither will your Father forgive your trespasses.' " He flipped a page. " 'And why beholdest thou the mote that is in thy brother's eye, but considerest not the beam that is in thine own eye?' " More pages rustled. " 'Judge not, and ye shall not be judged: condemn not, and ye shall not be condemned: forgive, and ye shall be forgiven.' Refusing to forgive is just as much a sin. When are you going to let go?"

Conner wanted to say never but knew that wasn't right. He

didn't like William beating him over the head with scripture verses. "I can forgive, but that doesn't mean I have to see her or talk to her."

"But you haven't. You haven't forgiven your mother for being the person she was, so you can't forgive Vivian for being the person she was forced to be."

"She had choices just like we all have."

"But sometimes you get pushed so far you can only see one choice."

"There is always a right choice, always."

"Randolph told me something once I refused to believe, but now, seeing the hatred in your eyes, it might be true. He told me that you hated your mother so much that you thought about killing her. He wanted to save you from that and so got you that job on the ship to take you away."

Conner clenched his hands into fists. "I wouldn't have done it."

"Are you sure? If you were pushed to the point you thought you had no other choice?"

Defeated, he sagged in his chair. "Yes, I'm sure." A man his mother brought home had been slapping her around. He'd stepped in to protect her. The man left and his mother had been furious with him for losing her the money that man would have paid. She'd said it was all part of it and started hitting him. He'd found his hands around her throat but couldn't squeeze. He just held his hands there, and she laughed at him. He'd left and gone to Randolph, who smuggled him on board the ship he worked on. No, as much as he hated his mother, he could never kill her. The years had cooled his anger, and his hatred had turned to loathing pity, then apathy. But never forgiveness.

"Vivian's choices were to become a prostitute or to die not knowing the Lord. I'm not condoning what she did, but becoming a prostitute afforded her the time to meet her Lord and Savior, thus saving her soul from eternal damnation. She would rather die now than go back to that life. Separate the sin from the sinner."

"I don't want to talk about Vivian or my mother."

"You have to forgive them sometime."

Did he? "Tell me about your wife and child."

Thankfully, William allowed the change in conversation. It was almost like having Randolph back, at least in his looks. It was very late before William left, and Conner spent the remainder of the night tossing in his bed. If he'd gone back, would he have tried to kill his mother again? He didn't know. How could a son come so close to doing something like that?

He raked his hands into his hair. *Heavenly Father, forgive my unforgiving spirit.* He felt no relief in that prayer.

❧

At breakfast, Sarah was incensed. "He won't forgive her at all?"

William wiped the last of his egg yolks up with his toast. "Give him time."

"You said that five days ago when you went to talk to him that first night."

"His wounds go back to when he was a little boy."

"So do yours."

William pulled his eyebrows down but didn't counter.

Vivian sat quietly. She had allowed a small portion of hope to seep into her heart that William would be able to change Conner's mind. "I'm going to move to Seattle or Port Angeles and get a job." Her voice came out as small as a little child's.

"You can't." Tears immediately filled Sarah's eyes.

She wanted to cry, too, but no tears came. She felt numb inside. "I can't stay here. It hurts too much to be this near him and know he hates me." She stood and left the room. She didn't want to hear any arguments for why she should stay. She'd thought Sarah and William being here would bring her joy, but knowing she would lose them, too, by moving away just deepened her sorrow.

&

A young brunette woman entered Conner's store and approached Martin behind the counter. "I'm looking for Mr. Jackson."

He was near enough so he answered. "I'm Conner Jackson."

She gave him a smile that didn't reach her eyes. This stranger seemed to be mad at him, but he didn't know why. "I'm Mrs. William Carlyle."

"It's a pleasure to meet you." William had chosen well.

"I wanted to meet the unforgiving cad who broke Vivian's heart."

So it wasn't going to be a pleasure meeting her. "Would you like to come into the back?" If this woman was going to give him an earful, he didn't want it to be in front of Martin, Todd, and his customers.

"I just came to give you this." She opened her reticule and pulled out a rock.

He flinched, not knowing if she was going to throw it at him.

She handed it to him.

"What's this for?"

"It's the first stone." She turned and walked out.

He stared at the rock in his hand, still asking himself the same question, what was it for?

"What did she give you?" Martin asked.

"A rock." He turned the rock over into his other hand. On the backside was written *St. John 8:1–11*. He tucked it into his pocket.

That night after he'd gotten ready for bed, he took the rock along with his Bible and sat on the edge of his bed. He'd been curious all day about the one passage from God's Word she'd chosen. Fred jumped out of the box with her three sleeping pups and crawled up next to him. What one passage had Mrs. Carlyle thought would make a difference? He'd read the whole Bible. If this passage hadn't made a difference before, why would it now? He opened his Bible and began to read:

> *Jesus went unto the mount of Olives. And early in the morning he came again into the temple, and all the people came unto him; and he sat down, and taught them. And the scribes and Pharisees brought unto him a woman taken in adultery; and when they had set her in the midst, they say unto him, Master, this woman was taken in adultery, in the very act. Now Moses in the law commanded us, that such should be stoned.*

Conner slammed his Bible shut and stared at the cover. He didn't want to read anymore. A stirring in his spirit told him this would change his life. It *would* make a difference. If he finished the passage, he could never go back to his old way of thinking, his old way of not forgiving.

Fred pawed his arm and whined.

"I don't want to read it." He didn't want to forgive. Forgiveness was for those who deserved it.

Fred tilted her head sideways.

He tossed his Bible onto his bed and strode across the room to the window. The dark, moonless night reflected his empty soul. After a while, he went back to his bed, compelled to open the Bible again:

> *Now Moses in the law commanded us, that such should be stoned: but what sayest thou? This they said, tempting him, that they might have to accuse him. But Jesus stooped down, and with his finger wrote on the ground, as though he heard them not. So when they continued asking him, he lifted up himself, and said unto them, He that is without sin among you. . .*

Conner choked on these words.

> *Let him first cast a stone at her.*

Conner squeezed his eyes shut for a moment, then continued:

And again he stooped down, and wrote on the ground. And they which heard it, being convicted by their own conscience, went out one by one, beginning at the eldest, even unto the last: and Jesus was left alone, and the woman standing in the midst. When Jesus had lifted up himself, and saw none but the woman, he said unto her, Woman, where are those thine accusers?

"Right here," Conner said aloud.

Hath no man condemned thee? She said, No man, Lord.

"I have," Conner whispered.

And Jesus said unto her, Neither do I condemn thee: go, and sin no more.

Conner took a deep cleansing breath. " 'He that is without sin among you, let him first cast a stone at her.'" Jesus was the only one who had the right to condemn and stone that woman, but He didn't. Instead, He released her from her burden of sin; He sent her away to start her life anew. He didn't wait for her to confess her sin or ask for forgiveness. He just gave her a new start.

Conner thought of the men eager to condemn her. " 'And they which heard it, being convicted by their own conscience, went out one by one.'"

He looked at the rock, then read again, " 'He that is without sin among you, let him first cast a stone at her.'" He squeezed the rock in his hand. Sarah had given him the first stone to throw at Vivian. He was only permitted to throw it if he were without sin. He let the rock fall to the floor, dropped his head into his hands, and cried.

He wept for the loving mother he'd always wanted but had never had. He wept for hating the mother he did have. He wept for Vivian. And he wept for disappointing his Savior. Jesus had died for his sins. Jesus had died for Vivian's sins. And Jesus had died for his mother's sins. He was just as unworthy of the Lord's forgiveness as his mother. Perpetual sinners.

But Vivian was more worthy than them all. She had done as the Lord commanded and gone and sinned no more.

"Forgive me, Jesus."

"Neither do I condemn thee: go, and sin no more."

"Thank You, Lord."

"Go."

nineteen

The next day, Vivian sat in a chair on the back lawn with baby Vivian in her arms. "She's so precious."

Sarah beamed at her daughter. "I'm hoping we have a boy next."

"Are you in a family way?"

"You asked me that a week ago when we arrived. No. At least not yet. But we have this big house to fill now."

"I can see you running all over this yard, chasing after a dozen children." Her heart ached for the same future.

"I can't do it without you. You have to stay."

"Sarah, I can't." It would be easier on her and easier on Conner. He shouldn't have to live every day wondering if he was going to run into her. And he shouldn't have to avoid visiting his old friend because of her presence.

She would write and make a few inquiries about domestic positions in Port Angeles. It wasn't too far away, but far enough, and she could visit more easily. William had gone to her attorney and deeded her half the house. He said he would pay her for her share when he could. So she had gone down and deeded her share to baby Vivian. William shook his head and gave up.

William told her she was being silly. Maybe she was, but she didn't want anything to tie her to Port Townsend. . .and keep her near Conner.

"Vivian, you have a visitor," William said as he strode across the lawn with Conner.

She sucked in her breath at the sight of him. Conner looked neither happy nor mad. She wished she could read his intention. His coat hung heavy on him, pulling down at the shoulder seams as though under a great weight, and his pockets bulged.

Conner nodded to Sarah. "Mrs. Carlyle." Then he turned to her. "Vivian."

"Conner." She could see a rock clenched in his right hand. What was he going to do? She handed baby Vivian back to Sarah.

William held out his hand to his wife. "Let's go inside and give them some privacy."

Sarah's eyes widened. "But—"

William took the baby and helped his wife to her feet. The three left, and Vivian was alone with Conner. . .and the rock.

Conner stood no more than a foot in front of her. "Mrs. Carlyle came to me yesterday and gave me this." He opened his hand to reveal a rock the size of a fat plum. "She wrote St. John 8:1–11 on it. That's the story of the woman caught in adultery, and this is to be the first stone cast."

She glanced toward the house where Sarah had gone. What had Sarah been up to? Why give Conner a rock to stone her? She heard a thump. He'd dropped the rock on the ground at her feet.

"That was for treating you poorly these last few weeks." He pulled a rock from one of his bulging pockets. "This one is for not forgiving you." It fell to the ground, and he pulled out another rock. "This one is for hating you. I don't hate you anymore."

Forgiveness was one thing, but could he accept her back into his life? Would he still want to marry her? "Conner."

"Let me finish. Please. I have my pockets full." He pulled his coat front aside to reveal bulging pants pockets.

He went through a long list of foolish childhood sins. Rocks of various sizes littered the small patch of grass between their feet. Conner's accumulated sins lay discarded at her feet. But how did he feel about her?

He pulled out a particularly heavy rock the size of an

apple. "This one is for my mother. For everything she is and everything she's not." The stone hit the toe of his boot and rolled toward her.

Tears welled in her eyes. She knew that that one was hardest for him. His mother had wounded him as a little boy, a wound that had never healed over the years. Now maybe it could.

Conner moved the stones aside from in front of her with his feet, then knelt on the ground. He took her hand and put one last rock into it, a rock the size of the one he'd used for his mother. "This one is for you to use. I have been so wrong. My heart was hardened. Please forgive me for being unforgiving. For not forgiving you." Agony etched every line of his face.

She dropped the rock. It thudded onto the grass. "Of course I forgive you."

"Thank you."

Was there more? Would he say it? "Do you still love me?" She heard herself say, her heart aching to know.

He smiled wide. "More than ever. When I came here, I wasn't sure I could say that, but when I looked at you across the yard, I knew I'd spend the rest of my life loving you whether you loved me back or not."

She scooted forward in her chair and threw her arms around his neck, knocking him off balance and her, as well. His arms came around her as they both tumbled to the lawn.

She started laughing. "I'm sorry." She tried to get up.

"I'm not." He kept his arms securely around her. "I'm not letting you get away." He put his hand behind her head and lowered it until he could kiss her. Then he rolled her onto her back. "I'm not perfect and I'm doomed to make more mistakes." His head was framed by the clear blue sky.

"We all make mistakes."

"I'm going to San Francisco. I'm going to find my mother. When I get back, I'm going to propose to you again."

"I'll say yes."

He smiled. "You aren't supposed to answer yet."

"I didn't want you to have any doubt I'd be here when you got back. What are you going to say to your mother?"

"I'm not sure. I'll tell her that I forgive her."

"Are you expecting her to have changed?"

He shook his head. "But I need to see her face-to-face and tell her I forgive her. If I can do that, then I believe I can be a good husband to you."

"And if you can't?"

"I have to. I don't want to live without you."

"We could marry first, and I could go with you." She didn't want to chance losing him.

"This is something I have to do on my own."

"I'll start making wedding plans while you're gone. Shall we plan for the day after you return?"

"You're still in mourning clothes."

"I won't be starting this afternoon." She'd been in mourning garb long enough to honor Randolph. It was time to put the past to rest once and for all. "If you'll let me up, I have something I want to show you."

❧

Conner stood and helped her to her feet but kept his arms around her. "I know this is going to sound bold, but I always knew I could have just about any lady I desired. I have prayed every day that the Lord would keep that temptation from me. Then I met my best friend's wife, and my heart started on an impossible journey. I never thought I'd have you in my arms, and now I'm reluctant to let you go."

Vivian laid her head on his chest, and he felt complete at last. His other half. The Lord had given him another chance and blessed him with love. He released her and helped her back into her chair, then sat in one next to it. "You wanted to show me something."

"It may change everything."

"Only God can change *everything*."

She took a letter from her pocket and handed it to him. "Randolph's letter to you?"

She nodded. "You may read it."

Both the envelope and letter inside were a bit rumpled. Had she read this often? He unfolded it and read the first paragraph. "You told Randolph about your past?"

"It's why we fought the night he left."

He nodded and continued reading. When he finished, he folded it but didn't say anything. How did she think this would change everything? "What does this change?"

"He couldn't forgive me. He was going to send me away."

"That was Randolph. I have already forgiven you. I would like to think in time Randolph would have come around, but I don't know."

"Something else, too." She looked away as though nervous. "I have been married twice without having any children. I might be barren. What if I can't give you children?"

He took her by the upper arms and turned her back to face him. "I don't need children as long as I have you."

"Are you sure?"

"Yes. We'll just have to see what the Lord brings." He didn't want to hear further excuses, so he kissed her.

❧

Conner spent a week in San Francisco following leads to find his mother. His search ended at the Place of Hope Asylum. He was ushered into the administrator's office by a woman in full black nun's habit. He shook hands with a Mr. Clark and sat across the desk from the small man in a blue wrinkled suit. Suspicion squinted through the thick lenses of Mr. Clark's spectacles, making Conner feel as if he were being assessed for signs of mental illness.

Mr. Clark dipped the end of his pen into an inkwell. "Name of patient?"

"Bertha Jackson."

Mr. Clark wrote on the paper in front of him. "Symptoms?"

"I don't know."

"How am I to know if our facility is right for"—he looked down at his paper—"Bertha, if you don't tell me anything about her?"

"I was hoping you could tell me. I was told she might be here."

Mr. Clark lowered his glasses on his nose. "You're looking for someone who's already been committed here? Incredible. Rarely does anyone visit. Once the insane are dumped off here by either the state, a family member, or anonymously, they are forgotten by the outside world."

"Is she here?"

Mr. Clark removed his glasses and pinched the bridge of his nose as though gaining patience to answer. "We have over two hundred patients. I don't know every name. It'll take a search of our files. It takes a lot of time to run this facility." He stood and showed Conner to the door. "Sister Mary Agnes, would you help Mr. Jackson find out if we have the patient he is inquiring about?"

The stoop-shouldered nun smiled. "Come this way." She stopped at a door with a small pane of glass in it. "This is one of our women's wards." She motioned for him to look through the window.

Iron beds lined both sides of the room and ran down the middle. There was barely room to move between them. The women wore plain gray dresses that hung straight and loose. He searched for a woman who could be his mother. "Is she in there?"

"We have four more women's wards and two men's wards. Give me a name, and I'll know which ward. I know every person ever committed to this asylum."

"Bertha Jackson."

Sister Mary Agnes smiled. "I remember Bertha May. Come with me."

He was both nervous and relieved. *Lord, help me forgive her.*

He had no choice. No matter how vile she still was or what insults she might fling at him, he *had* to forgive.

Sister Mary Agnes led him to a small office with a desk and filing cabinets. Along the opposite wall was an iron bed like that in the ward. She offered the chair to him. He remained standing. How could he sit while an old woman stood? Was this the sister's room? Did she live here?

She pulled a file from the middle drawer of one of the cabinets. "I am good with names and faces but terrible with dates." She opened the file. "Bertha was with us from January of 1884 until December 5, 1893."

His mother had come to this place a few months after he'd run away, and left more than six years ago. This wasn't the end of his search, just a bend in his journey. "She was here for ten years? Why was she here? Where did she go?"

"I'm sure you have many questions. Where to begin?" Sister Mary Agnes returned the file to the drawer. "Shall we walk the grounds?" She guided him outside.

A small fenced courtyard contained several patients walking around or sitting. His mother had once been in that courtyard.

"Bertha was brought to us by city officials. She'd been badly beaten and was at the hospital first. She wouldn't tell anyone her name. For days all she would do was cry and rock. They kept her in a hospital ward until she attacked a nurse. Then they took her to the jail. The jail staff didn't want to deal with her so they brought her to us."

His mother was insane. Had she always been so? She would tell him how useless and what a burden he was one day, and the next, she'd buy him a useless gift instead of food to fill his empty belly. He never knew what mood she was going to be in. One time, she'd looked at him with this blank stare and asked him who he was.

"When she first arrived, we didn't know her name and kept her separate from the other patients. She would spend most of the day crawling around the room and under her bed, looking for something, muttering, 'My baby. I have to find my baby.' I made her a doll out of strips of cloth. I wouldn't give it to her until she told me her name. After that, she sat in the corner and rocked her baby. We slowly integrated her into the main ward. The only time we had any trouble with her was when someone would take her doll."

Sister Mary Agnes stopped at a wrought iron fence on the far side of the grounds and pinned him with a stare. "She named her doll Conner."

He widened his eyes. "How did you know my given name?"

The nun smiled. "I didn't. Conner is the name she gave her doll."

Did this mean that in some strange way his mother had loved him? "Where did she go?"

"I'm afraid she didn't leave." Sister Mary Agnes pointed beyond the fence. "She passed on from this life. She's in row three, plot seven."

He struggled to take in a breath as though someone had punched him in the gut. His mother was dead? He'd never considered that his search would conclude with news of her death. He stared over the fence to the grass beyond but could see no markers. He turned to Sister Mary Agnes, but she was halfway back to the building.

He made his way along the fence to the gate and entered. Small plaques in the ground marked burial sites. He turned at row three and stopped halfway down:

Bertha May Jackson
1850 – December 5, 1893

"I wasn't expecting this. I really thought you'd still be alive. I always hated you for who you were and for your cruelty to me." He stared at the plaque for a long time. Then Vivian's face came to his mind. He had to do it. "I forgive you, Mother, for all the bad things you did." He laid a fist-sized stone on the marker. Written on the stone was St. John 8:1–8. Even though he now knew his mother had been insane, he still couldn't bring himself to tell her that he loved her. His forgiveness would have to be enough.

❧

Vivian watched from her bedroom window as she waited for Conner to ride up. He would be discussing business again with William. Since he'd returned from California nearly a week ago, he'd hardly talked to her, too busy with his store and working with William on the shipping business. He wouldn't talk about his visit with his mother. It couldn't have gone well, or he'd be in better spirits. It felt as though he was more distant from her now than when he'd found out about her past.

She'd moved into one of the smaller bedrooms so William and Sarah could have the larger suite. William had told her that Conner gave her half of his portion of the shipping business and that was where the money was coming from that was put into her bank account each month. The money didn't matter if Conner wouldn't speak to her.

She watched him ride up and dismount from his horse. She took a deep breath and smoothed her dress before descending the staircase in a ladylike glide. Maggie stood by the door, but Conner wasn't there.

"Where's Conner?"

"He's waiting for you in the parlor." Maggie returned to the kitchen.

Vivian entered the parlor. "Conner."

His gaze drifted from the fireplace to her. "You asked to see me?"

He stood stiff and aloof. Why was he being so distant? There was so much to say and ask. She didn't know where to begin. "Why are you avoiding me?" The question came out without her actually choosing it.

"I'm not avoiding you." His expression was flat, as though someone had taken the life out of him.

Her emotions were all a jumble. "You are, too," she blurted out. "You come and talk to William but not me." She didn't want to be angry with him, but her words came out that way.

"I've been busy."

Busy staying away from her. "Is our wedding off?"

He raked a hand through his hair. "I think that would be best."

Her heart struggled to beat. He couldn't mean that. He'd forgiven her. "My sins are too much for you to bear."

A shadow of grief crossed his features, and he crossed the room to take her hand. "No. It's not you."

"Then what?"

"It's my mother."

"You found her, then?"

He released her and turned back to the empty fireplace. "Sort of. She's dead."

She put a hand on his arm. "I'm so sorry."

He looked down at her hand, then pulled away. "She died in an insane asylum. She was touched in the head."

"Conner, I'm so sorry." Facing his back, she touched his shoulder.

He jumped away from her. "They say insanity runs in families. I could go insane, too. I'm trusting the Lord to spare me, but I won't burden you with that."

She took three steps forward to stand as close to Conner as she could without touching him, tilted her head back, and looked up at him. "You are not insane."

"How can you have such confidence?"

She touched her chest. "I know it in here. You have Christ in you. You wrestle daily with trying to make right decisions. You are an honorable man who humbled himself to forgive the mother who hurt you terribly."

"But there is still a chance I could go crazy, just like her."

She put her fingers to his lips. "You won't. You are the most levelheaded, sane person I've ever met. We will trust in God to help us handle whatever circumstances we might be faced with. The only crazy thing I can think of that you might do is not marry the woman you love. You do still love me?"

A smile tugged at his mouth. "Every minute of every day." He pulled her close and kissed her.

twenty

June 1 was a beautiful, sunny day. The rhododendrons were in full boom. The small wedding took place in the backyard of the Carlyle House. Guests included Sarah and William and baby Vivian; Maggie and Scotty; Martin Zahn; Abigail Parker and her son, Harry; Peter and the other children from the orphanage; Finn; and a handful of other guests. Peter's aunt agreed to take him with the dog, and Finn had volunteered to accompany the five-year-old to the other side of the state. Finn said it was time for him to be moving on. He and Peter would leave the following day for Spokane.

Vivian waited anxiously to be signaled forward. She wore a cream dress with lavender flowers embroidered on it. William held out his elbow for her. "It's time."

She looped her hand through the crook in his arm and walked with him down the short aisle to where Conner stood. She could hardly believe this day was finally here and she was a June bride. After they had said their vows and exchanged rings, the minister gave Conner and Vivian a moment for another exchange they had requested. Conner handed her a white rock. "To always remember I'm a sinner and need to be forgiven daily."

She smiled. He'd found a truly white rock and had been thinking like she had. She pulled out a stone she'd painted white to show that they were cleaned white as snow by Jesus' blood. She handed the rock to Conner. "To always remember that I have been forgiven."

The minister pronounced them man and wife, and Conner kissed her.

The reception was held in the backyard, too, and the

children had fun running around. After all the guests had left, only Vivian and Conner, Sarah and William remained.

Conner dangled a key in front of her face. She spun to face him and reached for the key. "What's this for?"

He snatched the key out of her reach and pocketed it. "Close your eyes, and I'll show you."

She closed them and covered them with her hand.

He put his hand over hers and guided her around the yard.

She trusted him not to let her fall or get hurt. She was trying to figure out where in the yard she was but finally gave up.

He kept turning her around and making her walk in different directions. He finally stopped her on what felt like a paving stone and turned her to face something. "Open your eyes."

Before her stood the white house next door to Sarah and William's blue one.

"I didn't want you to have to live above the store, so I bought you a house."

"We'll be neighbors and can spend our days together raising our children." Sarah stood next to her.

Conner scooped Vivian up into his arms and carried her across the threshold. "Welcome home." He set her down inside, kicked the door closed, and kissed her.

Her brand-new life had begun.

A Letter To Our Readers

Dear Reader:

In order that we might better contribute to your reading enjoyment, we would appreciate your taking a few minutes to respond to the following questions. We welcome your comments and read each form and letter we receive. When completed, please return to the following:

Fiction Editor
Heartsong Presents
PO Box 719
Uhrichsville, Ohio 44683

1. Did you enjoy reading *The Captain's Wife* by Mary Davis?
   ❏ Very much! I would like to see more books by this author!
   ❏ Moderately. I would have enjoyed it more if

   _____

   _____

   _____

2. Are you a member of **Heartsong Presents**? ❏ Yes ❏ No
   If no, where did you purchase this book? _____

   _____

3. How would you rate, on a scale from 1 (poor) to 5 (superior), the cover design? _____

4. On a scale from 1 (poor) to 10 (superior), please rate the following elements.

   ____ Heroine   ____ Plot
   ____ Hero   ____ Inspirational theme
   ____ Setting   ____ Secondary characters

5. These characters were special because? _____

_____

_____

6. How has this book inspired your life? _____

_____

_____

7. What settings would you like to see covered in future
Heartsong Presents books? _____

_____

_____

8. What are some inspirational themes you would like to see
treated in future books? _____

_____

_____

9. Would you be interested in reading other **Heartsong
Presents** titles? ❏ Yes ❏ No

10. Please check your age range:
❏ Under 18   ❏ 18-24
❏ 25-34   ❏ 35-45
❏ 46-55   ❏ Over 55

Name _____

Occupation _____

Address _____

City, State, Zip_____

VIRGINIA
BRIDES

3 stories in 1

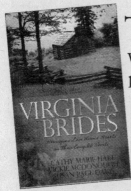

Traverse through Shenandoah Valley history. . .and love. When love starts to grow, will life's complications be too much to overcome? Can God bring good out of lives that seem to be spinning out of control?

Historical, paperback, 352 pages, 5³⁄₁₆" x 8"

Please send me ____ copies of *Virginia Brides*. I am enclosing $6.97 for each.
(Please add $3.00 to cover postage and handling per order. OH add 7% tax.
If outside the U.S. please call 740-922-7280 for shipping charges.)

Name_____

Address _____

City, State, Zip _____

To place a credit card order, call 1-740-922-7280.
Send to: Heartsong Presents Readers' Service, PO Box 721, Uhrichsville, OH 44683

Heart♥ng

HISTORICAL ROMANCE IS CHEAPER BY THE DOZEN!

Any 12 Heartsong Presents titles for only $27.00*

Buy any assortment of twelve *Heartsong Presents* titles and save 25% off of the already discounted price of $2.97 each!

*plus $3.00 shipping and handling per order and sales tax where applicable.
If outside the U.S. please call
740-922-7280 for shipping charges.

HEARTSONG PRESENTS TITLES AVAILABLE NOW:

(If ordering from this page, please remember to include it with the order form.)

Presents

Great Inspirational Romance at a Great Price!

Heartsong Presents books are inspirational romances in contemporary and historical settings, designed to give you an enjoyable, spirit-lifting reading experience. You can choose wonderfully written titles from some of today's best authors like Wanda E. Brunstetter, Mary Connealy, Susan Page Davis, Cathy Marie Hake, Joyce Livingston, and many others.

When ordering quantities less than twelve, above titles are $2.97 each.
Not all titles may be available at time of order.